CLASS OF LOVE

SIGN OF LOVE BONUS STORY INCLUDED
LETTERS FROM HOME SERIES

MARYANN LITTON

CLASS OF LOVE

Letters From Home Series

By
Maryann Jordan

Class of Love (Letters From Home Series)
Copyright 2017 Maryann Jordan

Cover Design by: Sommer Stein
    Editor: Shannon Brandee Eversoll
    ISBN: 978-0-9975538-9-5

DEDICATION

As a high school counselor, I worked with many students who joined the military after high school. A few of them I stayed close to and watched as they matured during their enlistment. I know letters from home meant so much to them and they were the idea behind these stories. For those, and all who have served, I dedicate this story to them.

Author Notes

When writing military romance, I do a lot of research in my desire to accurately portray the soldiers' jobs, duties, and situations, but know that in some areas I will fall short simply because I have never walked in their boots. I hope my readers will focus on the love story, while appreciating the service our men and women in the military.

DFAC – Dining Facility
ACU – Army Combat Uniform
MWR – Morale, Welfare, and Recreation
bird – helicopter

CHAPTER 1

(SEPTEMBER – ETHAN)

Tan. Brown. Khaki. Beige.

In Afghanistan, the color scheme rarely changed for someone in the Army. Good for camouflage...bad for morale. I'd been here for six months and the rest of my tour loomed long and hard in front of me.

I jogged along the wide, dirt path between the large, tan tents, the Moon Dust swirling with every step of my boots. The sand-colored powder that covered the ground, kicked up with the wind, our steps, and the movement of every vehicle.

Looking down the long row of tents, each one was almost the same as the next. Same color, generally the same shape. Everything here was bland...the dusty road, the tents, the sky when the wind blew, and even our clothes. I sometimes wondered if the monotony of our world was to match the monotony of our duties.

Coming to the tent I shared with my squad, I kicked the dust off my boots before I darted inside, glad to be out of the burning sun. The heat was oppressive, bearing down with a blistering intensity that made you want to hustle to get where you were going while at the same time zapping you of all strength.

It was only when you stepped inside that the differences in the tents became evident. Each side of ours was lined with three metal bunk beds, footlockers at the ends and tall metal lockers in between. I felt lucky to have a small tent. Lots of soldiers were packed in tents with twenty or more bunks. Hell, ours even had mattresses where some bunks were barely more than cots. Sparse compared to most people's standards, but over here, we learned to take our advantages wherever we could find them.

The floors were wooden, scuffed and worn planks. Not very aesthetic but better than just the dirt. We also had air conditioning and heat—a real luxury considering the weather in this country.

This tent held my squad and was not too far from the airfield where we worked. We had a card table in the middle, often used for poker nights. Pictures were taped to some of the lockers...wives, families, girlfriends, pinups. A couple of strings of drying laundry crisscrossed the space as well. Walking past the first two bunk beds, I came to mine in the back corner. That was another small advantage. I had the side and back wall next to my lower bunk, giving me a sense of privacy.

When I first came to Afghanistan, I had the front top bunk and as soon as the squad member with the back corner rotated home, I claimed dibs on his space. I didn't have any pictures taped to my locker—no wife or girlfriend, and hell, my old man sure as shit didn't deserve a place there.

Jerking my hat off my head, I ran my hand over my short hair, noting it was almost time to get it cut again. Deciding to take care of that later in the week, I nodded at the few members already in the tent as I stopped at my bed. A large, padded envelope lay on my blanket, assumedly left there by my best friend and bunkmate since he had gone to the mail tent. Looking over at Jon, I tilted my head in question, observing him opening up a large box.

"What the hell is this?" I asked, continuing to watch as he dug into the now open box, pulling out several well-packed bags of cookies.

Jon shot me a victory grin as he ripped open a bag and shoved a homemade cookie in his mouth. Answering while chewing, he replied, "We got these in the mail. You know... shit sent to soldiers. They were giving these out at the MWR."

The MWR—Morale, Welfare, and Recreation—was located in a large tent containing a library, computers, pool tables, and games. They gave out whatever they could to keep up morale. The Army tried to make us forget we were fighting a war on the other side of the world, but there was only so much they could do.

Shifting my gaze between the large box on Jon's bunk and the much smaller envelope on mine, I pressed, "And how did you get the box of cookies and I get this?"

Grinning with another cookie stuck halfway in his mouth, he replied, "Told you I was getting the mail. I was there first, so I get the goodies and you get what's left." Swallowing a large bite, he added, "Seems fair to me. You know, finders keepers and all that shit."

I shook my head while grumbling, "You're a selfish fucker, you know that?" Sitting down on my bunk, I ripped opened the padded, yellow, wrinkled envelope covered in smudges, and dumped the contents next to me on my bed. Well over a dozen folded pieces of paper dropped out and to make sure I had all the contents, I stuck my hand into the now empty envelope. Hearing Jon laugh, I looked up sheepishly. "Hell, I thought maybe they sent just one candy bar!"

"Quit whining, man," he joked as he tossed a bag of cookies over to me.

Catching the bag in mid-air, I grinned as I dug in greedily. The chocolate chip cookie was still slightly gooey, and the chocolate melted on my tongue. It wasn't as though I had not had a cookie while in Afghanistan, but a homemade one just tasted different...*better.*

The military tried to make things seem more like home, but where we were and what we were doing were always first and foremost on our minds.

Moaning in delight as I chewed another treat, I leaned back against my pillow, the pile of folded papers next to me. Picking up the first one, I unfolded it, my eyes quickly reading the carefully printed words.

Hi Soldier,

Our teacher said we need to thank you for your service. My name is Todd and our class will write to you all year. It is raining here. Does it rain there? We get a lot of rain and I hate it because we can't go outside. Staying inside during recess really ~~sucks~~ stinks. (my teacher made me take out the world suck). I had a grandfather who was in the Army and I saw his medals when we visited. Do you have any? Maybe you can send a picture of them if you have any. If not, maybe you'll do something to get one.

I looked up as a few other soldiers walked past us on the way to their bunks, eyeing the box Jon had as well. Grumbling, he tossed a small bag to one of them, growling, "That's it! The rest are for me!"

Grinning, I glanced back at the letter and thought that if I got shot, I could get a medal. Hope that's not what the kid wanted. Picking up another letter, my eyes scanned the contents.

Hello,

My name is Sarah and I am excited to be writing to a real live hero. My teacher says we get to write to you to make you happier. We are studying geography now and just learned where you are. It is really far away. I hope you are not missing home too much. I got to go to camp last summer and was away from my family for six weeks. I loved it but got homesick. I asked my teacher if she thought that you got homesick but she said I should ask you. So I will. Do you get homesick? She said we can send you goodies. What kind of treats do you like?

Unfolding the next one, I grinned at the careful print.

Dear Soldier,

My name is James. I got excited when our teacher told us what our classroom project is going to be. I've got an older brother in the Army and my dad was in the Air Force. My grandpa was in the Marines and he likes to say they are the best. But he is my mom's dad and my dad calls him an old jarhead. I don't know what that means, but it makes my grandpa mad and my brother laughs. So I laugh too. When I told my mom that we got to write to a soldier, she said that was wonderful. Then I told her I wanted to be a soldier too but she got mad. My teacher says we have to finish our letters now, so I will write more next time.

Each letter was similar and as I read them all, I noticed Jon staring at me, a wide-eyed dubious expression on his face. Looking over I barked, "What?"

"Do you have to answer all those? Hell, I woulda dumped them on someone else's bed if I thought there was nothing in there but letters."

Shrugging, I replied, "No worries, man. They're from a bunch of kids...kind of funny actually." And I realized those words were true. Hell, over here I'd take any diversion.

Jon's curiosity piqued and he stood, leaning over to snag one of the letters off my bed. Squinting, he said, "How the hell do you read this? God, it must be a boy's handwriting."

Picking up another one I nodded as I observed the penmanship. "Yeah, you can tell the girls' handwriting from the boys."

Jon, already bored, tossed the letter back to me before hiding the rest of the cookies in his footlocker and grabbing his toiletries. "Hittin' the shower," he called out as he headed through the front flap of the tent.

I found one neatly folded piece of paper, the handwriting clean and precise. *Gotta be the teacher.*

Hello,

I am the teacher of the fourth-grade class here at Eastville Elementary School, and we have chosen to write letters to a soldier for our class project this year. We will send monthly packets of letters to you – you do not need to answer each child, but we would love for you to just write the class as a whole when you are able.

We will be studying world geography and we already have pinpointed on our map where we have sent the letters. Any information you can give us about the terrain, weather...whatever you think the kids would like to know.

We would also like to know more about you. I know there is much you cannot share (and since these are fourth graders, there is much they don't need to know!), but we would love to hear about your life there.

We appreciate your service to our country and hope that we may provide you with a little bit of home. We would also like to send care packages to you, so feel free to let us know if there are certain things you need or just would like to have. Several of our

homeroom mothers are ready and willing to take cookie orders!
Hope to hear from you soon!
      Sincerely,
      Ms. Thompson

I sighed heavily as I pushed the notes back into the envelope. The idea of writing to a fourth-grade class held little appeal. *What the hell would I tell them?* I stood up and stretched, moving my head back and forth as my neck popped. Glancing at my watch, I saw it was almost time for dinner and I didn't intend to be late. I heard it was lasagna night and that was one thing the cooks could make and it tasted almost as good as the local Italian restaurant back home. And if they had garlic bread, I knew I'd have to be early to make sure they did not run out before I got there.

Looking back over my shoulder at my bunk, I grabbed the envelope full of letters and shoved it into my footlocker as some of the other soldiers called out greetings before we all headed out of the tent.

* * *

Four days later, finishing a long shift of backbreaking work, I stood underneath the water in the shower, the Moon Dust and grime washing away as my muscles relaxed for the first time that day. The helicopters had been flying almost non-stop and our work to keep them ready had seemed never ending.

Once clean, I shut off the precious water and toweled off, stepping out into the larger room, grateful to put on a clean Army Combat Uniform. The Afghan nationals who were employed in the laundry, kept our ACUs in top shape.

Jon finished shortly after and called out, "I hear they got a new Green Bean shop. Wanna check it out?"

The thought of fresh coffee made my mouth water as I agreed, anxious to try the new coffee shop. Entering the shop's tent, the scent of ground coffee beans drew us closer to the counter. Behind the counter I could see the espresso machine, bean roasters, and grinders. The long, wooden bar held bottles of various flavored syrups and while I'd never been a fan of flavored coffee, the smells assaulting my nose made me want to try all of them.

Seeing most of our team already there, sitting at picnic tables placed inside the tent, we made our way up the line, placing orders. The murmur of satisfied customers along with the rumble in my stomach had me anxious to wrap my hands around the cup of brew.

"You got any more of those cookies?" Jackson, one of our squad members, called out to Jon.

Hell, naw," he grumbled. "What I didn't share with you all, I ate in two days."

Many of the amenities on base were run by Afghan nationals and the Green Bean was no exception. The worker behind the counter grinned as he handed me the steaming cup of coffee and said, "Got cookies here!" He pointed to a basket of large, plastic-wrapped chocolate chip cookies.

Holding up two fingers, I threw more money down on the counter, picking up two of the cookies. Twisting around, I tossed one to Jon, saying, "Here you go. You shared with me, so I figure I owe you."

"Damn, man," Jon grinned, ripping the plastic off immediately and taking a bite before he even ordered his coffee. He continued to smile as he chewed, rolling his eyes up toward the heavens as though pondering the meaning of life.

"So, what's the verdict?"

"Fuckin' good, but they ain't made with love like those from home," he replied, still shoving more of the chocolate goodness into his mouth.

Laughing, I shook my head as I turned to walk over to a table that some of our squad had commandeered. The conversations droned on all around me, but my mind was elsewhere as I drank the fragrant brew. I'd chosen a caramel latte, not even worrying about my man-card and when I sat down and scanned the orders from my squad members, I knew they'd decided to sample the flavors as well.

While they talked, I could not get the letters from the kids out of my mind. I had intended to write a simple thank you, or even possibly share them with some other guys, figuring that between several of us, we could occasionally write back. After all, what the fuck could I say to a bunch of nine-year-olds?

"Where's your head?" I glanced up to see Tom staring at me, his eyes raised in question. "You're drinking that high-octane coffee and your mind is somewhere else."

Tom was a good friend and I was grateful he was not drawing undue attention to me. The last thing I wanted was for anyone to think my head wasn't in the game. Out here, keeping your wits about you could mean life or death.

"Just remembered something I have to do," I said as nonchalant as possible. Nodding to the others, I stood, tossing my now empty cup into the trash and grabbed a water bottle before heading back to my tent. A breeze was blowing and I was grateful it wasn't enough to kick up the dust. The relentless sun bore down and I almost regretted the hot coffee. Twisting the cap off the water, I chugged it eagerly.

Nodding to a few people I knew along the way, I passed the MWR, not interested in any of their offered activities today. Stepping inside my tent, I moved straight to my footlocker. Kneeling down, I opened it and found the large, stuffed envelope still lying on top. Grabbing it, I dumped the contents onto my bunk again, only this time I sorted the notes as I opened them. Grabbing a pad of paper, I wrote down the names of all the children, figuring if I was going to send just a thank you letter, I should add some personal comments as well.

An hour later I walked over to the mail tent, handing the newly addressed letter to the clerk. As I walked back out into the blistering sun, I grinned as I slid my sunglasses back onto my face.

CHAPTER 2

(OCTOBER – BROOKE)

There is something unnatural about a quiet elementary school classroom...and yet so welcoming to the teacher.

The children in my class were at their music session, giving me the opportunity to check my mailbox in the school office. Nodding at the school secretary as I passed her neatly organized desk, I made my way back to the hallway leading to the teacher's lounge. Bending to peek in my mailbox, I viewed the papers filling the small cubby and I pulled them out with little enthusiasm. I shuffled through them, walking back to my room. A catalog of classroom furniture, weekly announcements, a newsletter on educational learning opportunities, and a reminder about the upcoming professional development committee meeting. And an envelope...from an APO address.

Excitement slammed into me, growing with each step as I hastened down the hall. Entering my empty classroom, I tossed the other articles onto my desk, clutching the envelope reverently in my hands. *Oh, thank God!* The children had asked when we would hear back from a soldier, but I could do nothing but tell them we hoped someone got our letter who would write back.

Last summer, at an educational in-service for classroom projects, a former soldier had spoken about the morale-boosting effects of receiving items from home. He explained how many soldiers might not get anything from family or friends, but letters from children would often provide the emotional boost needed when working and serving in a war zone.

I was concerned at first, wondering how the children would respond to the idea of a soldier in a real-time war. Fourth graders are still children and I had no desire to take away their childhood with a project dealing with the effects of war. So the classroom project was a gamble, but the principal had been supportive...as long as I informed the parents. Ugh—that had been my greatest fear. But thank goodness, every parent signed the permission form for their child to participate. In fact, several had offered to help when needed.

Now, with shaky hands, I opened the envelope feeling the need to read the contents before the children came back into the room. After all, I might have to censor part of the letter to them, depending on what he or she said. My eyes scanned the neatly printed writing, and I could not help but smile at the formal letter.

Specialist Ethan Miller. My fingers automatically traced the words across the page, as the reality of him writing while half-way around the world struck me. Sucking in a deep breath, I finished the contents, now excited for the children to come back from their music class.

Sitting at my desk, I looked around the room. I loved my classroom, with the desks arranged in clusters of four and a reading corner filled with bookshelves of any books

I thought they would like to read. The windowsills were filled with the pots of plants we worked on last month. Halloween and fall decorations were taped to the walls, including the latest examples of their artwork. Carefully designed bulletin boards covered with both the children's work and learning tools hung on each wall. My desk, which I tried, but failed, to keep organized held a conglomerate of pens, pencils, papers, files, artwork, and knick-knacks given to me from students.

On one wall, a large world map hung, with our city marked with a large red push-pen and Afghanistan marked with a yellow one. For a moment, my mind wandered to where he was...so far from us.

Hearing the slight noise of children in the hall, I could not even jump up to hush them, my anticipation at such a high. Rushing to the door, I opened it and with only a raised-eyebrow-teacher-look, the children quieted as they entered the room.

Before they took their seats, I clapped my hands and said, "Okay, everyone, we've got a treat, so listen up." Once all eyes were on me, I reached behind me and picked up the envelope. Holding it for all to see, I announced, "We've got a letter back from our soldier friend."

The excitement was palpable as the children cheered and clapped. Raising my hand, in our signal for silence, they quieted, but the undercurrent vibration of anticipation was felt throughout the room.

"Okay, remember when you were in kindergarten and you got to sit in a circle around the teacher?" I asked, receiving nods from all the children. "Well, we're going to do that now, so come on up, find a place and let's gather around to see what he has to say."

The sound of chairs shuffling and little feet hastening to the front as excited voices whispered loudly filled the classroom. Soon, all twenty-four children were in a semi-circle around my chair and I smiled at their eager faces.

"Brad, would you go to the globe and point out where Afghanistan is?"

I watched as he stood, moving to the globe sitting on my desk, and spun it around a few times before landing his finger on the right country. "Good, good. Now, it is on the opposite side of the Earth, so is his time of the day the same as ours?"

Gaining the correct answer, I smiled at their attention and then pointed to Stan as he raised his hand.

"So when we're sleeping, he's working and when we're at school, he's sleeping?"

"Essentially, that's right," I replied. "Starting tomorrow, we'll be studying the solar system in our science lessons and we're going to talk about how the Earth rotates around the sun and how that makes day and night different for different sides of the world."

"But read the letter now!" begged Sarah, her impatience mirroring the other children's.

Nodding, I grinned. "Okay, okay. We have a letter from a soldier in the Army and his name is Ethan Miller." Unfolding the paper, I began to read.

Dear Ms. Thompson and class,

I was very glad to receive your letter and to have the chance to write to your class this year. I will try to answer some of the questions the students asked. I have been here for just over a year and have one more year in this tour of duty (that means my time here). I am originally from Roanoke, Virginia and love the mountains. But I have to admit, I love the beach as well. I notice you are from Chesapeake, VA, so I suppose you get to see the beach a lot.

I live in a tent filled with bunk beds. It's not very private, but we're usually just in here for sleep or some down time. There are twelve of us sharing this tent but some tents hold almost fifty soldiers. I have a small locker and a footlocker (like a little chest) that I keep my things in.

It's very hot here in in Afghanistan (where I am) in the summer – there are some cooler mountains but I'm not stationed there. Then in the winter, it gets really cold.

My job in the Army is to work as a mechanic. Most of what I do is here at the base but I do go out and work in the field. Yes, I do know how to shoot a gun and have one with me at all times.

Someone asked about the food – it's not too bad. Although sometimes it tastes bland and I really miss places like Pizza Hut and McDonald's. And a new coffee shop opened up so we can get fresh coffee. They also have chocolate chip cookies, which is a treat.

I don't really know what else to say right now, but thank you for the letters. If you write back, I promise to answer.

Sincerely, SPC Ethan Miller

The children's eyes, glued to me as I finished reading his letter, all blinked, almost in unison, before they clapped and comments abounded.

"I can't believe he sleeps in a bunk bed!" "We should send him chocolate cookies!" "He didn't tell us if he gets to shoot his gun!" "My dad works on trucks!" "Can he send us pictures?"

Lifting my hands, I shushed the children once more, and said, "Okay, find your desks and get ready to write. I'll give you twenty minutes to write your next notes to Mr. Miller and then after lunch we'll discuss what we would like to include in a box to him."

The children scrambled back to their desks, eager to have this project for their writing assignment for the day.

"Are you going to write to him also?"

Looking down at one of the girls in my class, Heather's large blue eyes staring up at me, I replied, "I suppose I should send a note as well."

Heather reached out and placed her small hand on my arm and said, "I think he would like it, Miss Thompson. You're awfully pretty and it would make him feel better if you wrote to him too."

Laughing, I patted her hand as she hurried back to her seat. Sitting down at my desk as the children wrote their notes, my mind wandered over her words. *Would he like a personal note? What would I say? What if he's married? That would seem weird.* But the more I thought about it, I decided that a friendly, pen-pal letter from an adult might be welcome. *He doesn't have to reciprocate.*

Forcing it out of my mind, I pulled out a stack of math homework papers and began to grade as the children worked eagerly on their letters.

* * *

"So, what's he like? Come on, Brooke, you can't keep secrets!"

Emily, my roommate, was shooting a Cheshire-cat grin toward me over her plate of Chinese food. We ordered in and the scent of sesame chicken, egg rolls, and fried rice filled our apartment. I had shared an apartment with her for two years, but she was getting married in the spring so I would need a new roommate—a daunting prospect.

My chopsticks halted in mid-lift on their way to my mouth and I stared back at her. "I have no idea," I replied.

"It's not like we got that personal in letters from a bunch of nine-year-olds!"

"Yeah, but you decided to write a more personal letter back." Emily pouted slightly, which only made her look more childlike. With her trim, petite figure and short black hair she appeared elfish and while I was only a few inches taller, my curves always made me feel so much bigger than she.

Shrugging, while taking a bite of egg roll, I said, "Don't know what he thinks. We haven't gotten a letter back yet. He might be old…might be married…might have five kids of his own." Chewing thoughtfully, I added, "And this is not some project to find a man! Geez, Emily…this is about the kids learning geography, world studies, politics, writing, and community service."

Rolling her eyes, she popped another piece of chicken into her mouth, before replying. "Aren't you the least bit interested in what kind of man decides to write to a bunch of kids?"

"One who's probably lonely and has a little bit of time on his hands," I replied, although secretly I knew that not everyone has the ability to relate to kids. "Anyway, it was only one letter. Who knows it he'll keep it up?"

We changed the subject, but now that she brought it up, I could not get Ethan Miller off my mind. After dinner, Emily headed out to meet her fiancé and I had the apartment to myself. I loved my space and felt lucky to have found the first-floor apartment with a killer view overlooking a neighborhood park. My apartment had been the model when the complex was built and had been fitted with upgrades all through the rooms. It shouldn't be hard to find a new roommate, but the idea of inviting a stranger to my comfortable corner of the world made me want to rethink my finances. *Maybe I can make it on my own!*

My mind easily slid back to the soldier as Emily's questions about him moved through my thoughts as well. Curiosity grabbed ahold of me and I sat down on the sofa with my laptop. *How can I write to him intelligently, if I have no idea what his life might be like?*

Clicking on my search, I started with a soldier's life in Afghanistan. I began with the images and viewed picture after picture of tan tents in perfectly straight rows. Some of the pictures showed the interiors and I scrolled through many of them, hitting print on the ones I thought the children would like the most. The starkness of the accommodations hit me and I looked up, my gaze moving around my apartment. *All of this for just me and Emily.* After absorbing the images, I moved to a few articles about life for U.S. soldiers in Afghanistan.

Later, as I lay in my bed, sleep not coming, I turned on the lamp on my nightstand. Padding over to my dresser, I opened the top drawer, pulling out a pad of paper and a pen. Crawling back into bed, I sat for a few minutes deep in thought of what to say. Sighing heavily, I finally began to write.

CHAPTER 3

(NOVEMBER – ETHAN)

The Boeing Apache helicopters, with forty-eight feet rotor diameters and fitted with their Longbow missiles, were a sight to behold lined up in the airfield. The dark, sleek bodies, ready to rain hellfire down on their targets never ceased to make me pause and view them with pride. Waspish in appearance, I knew at some time, a new breed of warbird would take the place of these, but that would be long after I was no longer in the Army. For now, these were the best we had and working on them made me feel as though I was involved in something important.

Jon and I had our hands inside the motor of one of them. The four-blade, twin turboshaft attack helicopter had a tailwheel-type landing gear arrangement and was equipped with a tandem cockpit for a two-man crew. It featured night vision systems and was heavily armed.

Cables ran from the electronics to our computer diagnostic system. Our job was to perform maintenance on the weapons components, fire control units, and sighting systems as well as all electronic and mechanical components. In other words...we kept the helicopters ready to fly at top capacity any moment. Thanks to us, the pilots just had to concentrate on their missions and not how their bird was performing.

Clearing the fire control system, I patted the side of the Apache, loving the mechanics of this flying armament. One of the pilots sat in the cockpit as we ran through the maintenance checks of the lighting and communication systems. By lunchtime, we cleared and armed several of the Apaches in our section, making them ready for their next mission.

The large hangar where we worked was cloth, suspended over the massive metal framework. Today we had it mostly closed off to keep the wind from tossing sand onto our instruments as we worked. Wiping my face, I glanced at my watch, glad to see the shift almost over.

"Hey Miller?"

The shout came from another buddy and I lifted my head from the electronics I was working on.

"Yeah?"

"I was just at the mail tent. Rogers said to tell you that you've got a package."

Jon looked over at me, his head tilted in question.

Shrugging, I replied, "Got no idea. God knows my old man isn't sending anything." Jon nodded, not asking any more. He already knew my mom had died the year before I graduated from high school. Dad, a car mechanic, fell into depression without mom. He worked, but that was about all. Every night after he got home, he opened up a can of anything he could microwave, ate and then sat in his old recliner in front of the TV. *Never even made it to my high school graduation.* I joined the Army a week after high school and here I was, six years later. *So, nope...no care package coming from my dad.*

"You think it could be from those kids who wrote to

you before?" Jon's question interrupted my musings concerning my old man. At his words, my thoughts perked up. A care package from a bunch of kids would probably have food in it. And more letters. I had no clue why the idea of more letters from a bunch of kids sounded good, but I could not stop the hope that filled my chest.

By the end of the day, I was ready for a shower, a meal, and a bed, but the desire to make it to the mail tent over-shadowed all other thoughts. I jogged along rows of dirt-tan tents, sandbags stacked at the entrance to each one. Making it to the one that distributed the mail for our platoon, I entered. The front section of the tent was bifur-cated with a long wooden counter. The back section, behind a tent flap, was where the shelves, stacks, and bins of incoming and outgoing mail was kept.

"Hey, Miller," came the greeting.

I smiled at the uniformed woman standing behind the wooden plank counter. "Howdy, Kerns," I greeted back. Her cute smile gave most men a hard-on when they came in for the mail, but she ignored them all. Her husband back in the states had her complete loyalty and so for us, she was just a good friend. "Hear I got something and you just can't wait to have me take it off your hands."

Laughing, Private Kerns replied, "Yeah, you got a nice sized box. Hang on." She turned and headed behind a flap into a rear room. A minute later she walked back, a card-board box at least eighteen inches long in her hands. "Looks like you got something from Brooke Thompson... ring a bell? She must be someone special to send some-thing to you," she joked.

Reaching for the box, I grinned. "She's a teacher at an elementary school in the states. I'm her class project."

Kern's smile faded as she said, "Oh, damn. And here I thought you had some hot chick sending you goodies!"

"Sorry to disappoint," I threw out, eager to get back to my tent to see what they sent. Walking away, I had to admit, I was curious about the teacher, having had a few hot-teacher dreams about her even while knowing she could be a married grandmother. *Well, hell...I can dream, can't I?*

Stepping inside my tent, I was glad that most of the squad was either in the showers or not back from duty. I set the box on the floor and pulling out a knife, sliced through the packing tape. Opening the top carefully, I peered inside. *Jackpot!*

I pulled out bags of Halloween candy, pumpkin spice cookies, chewing gum, supplies of deodorant, shampoo, toothpaste and, near the bottom, a folded t-shirt. Pulling out the x-large hunter green shirt, I turned it around, grinning as I saw Eastville Elementary Eagles emblazoned on the front, with a giant eagle, its wings spread in flight. It even looked like the shirt would fit.

Laying it to the side on my cot, I reached into the bottom of the box, pulling out the large envelope, stuffed full of what I hoped were letters. Funny, but while the treats were great, it was the letters that had my attention.

Grabbing out the first one, I unfolded the paper, once more recognizing the handwriting of a little boy.

Dear Mr. Miller,

It is nice to now have a name to put to the letter. I was excited to hear that you work as a mechanic. So does my dad. He's going to let me help him when I get older. If you get a chance to show us a picture of one of the trucks, I would like it. Maybe I can be a soldier when I grow up also. I hope you like the candy. Our class decided to share our Halloween candy with you. This is all I could write and the teacher is telling us it is time for lunch. Goodbye, Chad

Jesus, was I ever that young? I tried to remember the

fourth grade and visions of my older teacher, Mrs. Martsen came to mind. *Oh, she was a stickler for rules!* Opening another note, I laid back on my bunk and read.

Dear SPC Miller (our teacher told us how to write your name),

I hope you like the cookies. My mom and I made them. We didn't want to just send you some candy, but made our Thanksgiving cookies instead. I hope you get to have turkey on Thanksgiving. Do they have turkeys over there? If not, then maybe you can have a chicken. If you like the cookies, then let me know and I'll have mom make more. Chloe

Realizing I had never had a pumpkin spice cookie, I reached over to the bag and opened the zip-lock. The cookies had been carefully wrapped in the t-shirt and were still whole. As soon as the bag opened, I got a whiff of delicious pumpkin, nutmeg, and ginger. Taking a bite, I was transported back to before mom died, when she baked all the traditional foods for Thanksgiving, including pumpkin pie. Chewing slowly to savor each morsel, I leaned against the headboard of my bed, making sure to lick the crumbs off my fingers. *I gotta tell Chloe that her mom is a world-class baker.*

Dear Specialist Miller,

I really like that you have the word specialist in front of your name. Does that mean you are special at something? We have a special board in the room where our best work gets shown. Ms. Thompson says that you have to spend the holidays over in ~~Afgani~~ Afghanistan. I think that is a hard word to spell. I'll go to my dad's for Thanksgiving. He's got a new family now so I don't know if I'll have a good time. I get to stay at home for Christmas. Do you get to go home for Christmas?

I had just finished reading a few more notes, when Jon

poked his head in and yelled, "Come on. Get cleaned up. We're all going to the DFAC. They got turkey!" Others came in from their showers and the room began to fill. Thoughts of the dining facility had me stuffing the letters and goodies in my footlocker, deciding to finish reading them later when I had more privacy.

Grabbing my toiletries and towel, I ran to the showers, washing the dust and sand out of my hair and off my body. Within fifteen minutes, I joined Jon and my buddies in the service line. The scent of turkey and gravy, along with mashed potatoes filled the tent and looking around I knew the line was only going to get longer as soon as everyone figured out what they were serving. Reaching the end, I saw the desserts...pies. Looked like apple and pumpkin were left and I grabbed a slice of apple.

Weaving between the chairs, Jon and I made our way to where our squad was seated. Long rows of tables filled the room with bottles of condiments, salt, and pepper centered on each one.

Digging into dinner, Jon looked over and asked, "So who sent the package?"

Swallowing, I replied, "That class of kids. They sent some more cookies—"

"Homemade?" he interrupted, his expression mirroring a kid in a candy store. "You didn't eat them all already, did you?"

"Sure they're homemade and no, I didn't eat them all yet. But there's also Halloween candy."

"Fuck yeah, that's what I'm talking about!" he enthused.

As the conversation flowed all around me, I finished quickly. The desire to get back to finish reading the letters was overpowering. I didn't understand the need, but it was a welcome feeling nonetheless to have someone to connect with. During my tours, I'd been envious of the married soldiers as they received letters or emails from wives or kids. The ones who were engaged could really get on my nerves with all their lovey-dovey shit, and the pin-up photos of hot looking girlfriends.

I was even envious of the soldiers who got letters and packages from parents or siblings. Hell, with mom gone, no siblings, and a dad that didn't give a shit, that left me with no one back home to care enough to write. *Until now.*

Nodding toward Jon, I headed back out into the evening. The sun was setting over the mountains in the background. The sounds of the base all around were familiar and strangely comforting, but I looked forward to being back in the States. Sucking in a deep breath, I allowed myself to count down the months left on my tour. Seven months to go. As I arrived back at my tent, I immediately retrieved the envelope.

Dumping the entire contents onto my cot, I was surprised to find a picture that I had missed earlier, paper-clipped to the teacher's note. Holding up the picture, my eyes roamed over the class of children, their beaming faces pointed toward the camera. But it was the woman standing behind them that captured my attention.

Dark, chestnut hair, hanging down below her shoulders. Heart-shaped face. Pink lips posed in a wide smile. She must not be very tall since she was only a head taller than the boys standing in the back row. Each of her hands rested on the shoulders of the two boys nearest her. As my eyes reluctantly left her face, I noticed the relaxed smiles of the children. *I'll just bet she's a sweet teacher...not like Mrs. Marsten!*

Suddenly, now that I had a photograph, the letters seemed more real—they belonged to the faces I was staring at. Turning the picture over, I was thrilled to see the names of each child printed on the back. Now I could match up a note with a child. And there was her name. Brooke Thompson. *Brooke. Damn...that name matches that gorgeous face.*

Giving a mental shake, I reminded myself that she could be married...or engaged...or involved...or...*fuck, stop! She's just the teacher...nothing more!*

Opening her letter, I was unable to stop the smile, already recognizing her neat handwriting.

Dear SPC Miller,

I want to thank you for answering our notes. The class was thrilled to receive your letter and, as you can see, they have lots of questions.

I sent a picture of the class (I had their parents' approval) so this way you will be able to match up a child with their face. I wrote their names on the back for you. I thought perhaps it would seem more personal. And, if you are able to send a photograph of you, the children would love it.

The children have been busy with Thanksgiving activities and wanted to make sure that I got this out for you in time.

We would like to send you, and any of your friends, a Christmas box so please let me know what we can collect for you. We've been reading about what we can send and the children are very excited.

We are studying the geography, including the climate, of Afghanistan, so anything you have to say about those topics would be good also.

The children have been fascinated with the concept that your night is our day. They find is amusing that you are sleeping when they are in school and you are working when they are fast asleep. We have also been studying the solar system, particularly how the earth rotates and moves around the sun. We have a model in the room and that helps them to understand the different time zones.

Again, thank you for taking the time to share your experiences with us. Looking forward to hearing from you soon,

Brooke Thompson

I re-read the letter several times before pulling the class picture out again. Her smiling face seemed to reach across the continents and touch something deep inside. Sighing, I shook my head. *Damn! It must be the holidays that's got me so sentimental!*

Shoving the letters back into the envelope, I slid the class picture into the top of my footlocker so that every time I opened the lid, the image would be front and center for me to see. An idea hit my mind and I leaped out of my bed, jogging past the dozens of look-alike tents until I came to the communications center. Stepping inside, I was grateful to see a couple of empty computers. Sliding into the metal chair, I checked my email first. Firing off a quick note to my older sister, now married with a couple of kids, I then deleted most of the spam in my feed.

Typing in Eastville Elementary School, I was pleased when their website came up with teachers' pictures. Clicking on fourth grade, I saw her standing with four other women, all wearing the same T-shirt they had sent to me. Definitely petite, she was shorter than the others, but her smile was the same wide beam as the one with the children.

Glancing around to see if anyone was looking at my screen, I viewed everyone else's attention plastered to their own computers. Opening Facebook, I quickly typed in Brooke Thompson. There were quite a few, but narrowing it to Chesapeake, Virginia, her profile popped up.

My breath caught in my throat—her close-up profile picture was stunning. Green eyes, chestnut hair, and kissable mouth sent my libido into overdrive. I searched her relationship status—Single. I had no idea why I had fixated on her...*maybe I've been without a woman for too fuckin' long!* I spent several minutes clicking through her pictures, each one drawing me in further.

Closing down the computer, I walked back out into the night. The moon had risen over the horizon, the stars winking and, for a moment, I could close my eyes and almost pretend I was back home...anywhere but here.

Arriving at my tent, I nodded to Jon. Before he started bitching, I opened the footlocker and grabbed the pumpkin-spice cookies and tossed him the bag. Snatching them greedily, he began munching as I pulled out my paper and pen again, along with the kids' letters. With renewed vigor, I eagerly began answering their questions.

CHAPTER 4

(DECEMBER – BROOKE)

If I eat one more piece of fudge or divinity or fruit cake, I won't fit into my pants!

I walked into the teachers' lounge during lunch, staring at the amount of holiday food on the counter, and almost walked out. But before I could escape, the other teachers sitting at the table called out their greetings.

Plopping down into the empty chair, I pulled my salad from my lunchbox, determined to eat healthy for once. The conversation circled around the table, each person talking about their holiday plans.

"You heading to Tennessee?" Heather asked.

Shaking my head, I explained, "This year my parents are taking a holiday cruise, so I'll be spending the break here."

"You aren't going on the cruise with them? Oh, my God, I'd love to head to the Bahamas for the holidays."

The thought of white, sandy beaches, blue skies, and warm sunshine elicited moans from the others, along with incredulous looks shot my way.

"I know, I know," I nodded, spearing another piece of

tomato. "But this is my parents' thirtieth anniversary, and even though they invited me, I wanted them to have this time together." I didn't mention that while I loved my parents' company, the idea of being the third wheel on a romantic cruise did not appeal to me.

"So what are you going to do?" Jeannie asked, her eyebrows raised at the idea of me staying in town for the holidays.

"I'll just be at home," I replied sharply, then tempered my response with a smile. "It's fine...really. I'll have my own holiday traditions."

The conversation quickly turned from me and I gratefully shoved in the rest of my salad before making my way back to my class. The children had been bordering on unruly all week, their excitement about the holidays overflowing into our classroom. They kept asking about Specialist Miller, but so far we had no correspondence from him.

Sitting in my empty room for the few more minutes until my class returned, I heaved a sigh. I had not known how to answer their questions. *Is he safe? Is he healthy? How have I gotten emotionally invested over a couple of months with just a few letters?*

Hearing my door open, I looked up in surprise when the school secretary came in, a huge smile on her face. And in her hands...a thick envelope!

"Is that what I hope it is?" I asked, unable to keep the excitement out of my voice.

"I saw the mailman drop this off and I just had to bring it to you. Gloria has driven us crazy with wanting to hear from her soldier!"

The secretary's granddaughter, Gloria, was in my class and kept insisting to her grandmother that he would surely write before the holidays.

As she handed the envelope to me, I thanked her before ripping it open. Inside were two smaller envelopes. One was marked **For the Class** and the other marked **For Ms. Brooke Thompson.** *One for me?*

Before I had a chance to process the reasons for a separate letter, the children rushed in from lunch, their voices raised in pre-holiday break jubilation. Standing, I gave my best teacher-look to quiet them, its success only marginal. So instead, I held up the envelope and waited until their eyes took in what I possessed.

Cries of "he wrote!" and "finally!" filled the air. The children quickly moved into their semi-circle so that we could read it together.

Taking my seat, I opened the one for the class, smiling as I recognized his handwriting.

Dear Class,

I wanted to thank you for the holiday goodies you sent. I shared them with friends and became very popular! I also read each of your letters many times. It was nice to have so many letters from back home in the United States. I tried to keep up with your questions and will answer as many as I can.

I work on helicopters. The Army uses helicopters for lots of things and the ones I work on are special. My job is to make sure they are working correctly so when the pilots are ready to fly, everything goes perfectly. We call the helicopters "birds" but to me, they look like enormous wasps.

I do have good friends here. One of my bunkmates loves your goodies as well, and I have to hide some from him or he would eat them all! During our non-work time, we can play pool, football, get on computers, read, and there is a gym for us to work out.

I know you are studying geography so I will tell you that I can see mountains right outside my tent. I am in a valley, but it is very dry and dusty here. We don't get a lot of rain and there is very little grass where I am. It does rain here in the early spring and a little bit in the fall, but the late spring and summer are dry and hot. It can get well over 100 degrees in the summer months and close to 0 degrees in the winter. I see snow in the mountains but not at our base.

Your teacher said that she explained that I am on the opposite side of the world from you, so when you are asleep, I am working in the daylight and when it is night here, you are at school. My favorite time is night, when the stars and moon are very bright. That's when I can pretend I am back at home in Virginia.

I hope this letter gets to you before the holidays and that each of you has a very Merry Christmas. We do get to celebrate here as well. They serve us turkey and ham, as well as potatoes and we have lots of cakes. We eat in the DFAC, which means dining facility, which is like a big cafeteria. I do miss eggnog and my mom used to make a really good applesauce cake for the holidays.

I really appreciate the class picture you sent. I made sure to study the names so that when I write to you, I am thinking of your name with your face. I am sending a picture of me in my Army uniform and perhaps your teacher can post it somewhere so that you will remember me.

Happy New Year and I can't wait to hear from you again.

SPC Ethan Miller

With shaky fingers, I pulled out the picture, staring at it for a few seconds before the children began clambering for a view. Smiling, I stood and walked over to our map and pinned it next to Afghanistan. Lining the children up, I had them walk by, orderly, to see what he looked like, but have to admit, I could barely take my eyes off him.

He was dressed in the green Eastville Elementary t-shirt, his biceps bulging and his blue eyes twinkling as he smiled for the camera to capture. The children chattered as they passed by and immediately wanted to write back to him. Glancing at the clock, I decided that there was no other lesson worthier than their desire to send him notes... especially not in the last few hours before the holiday break.

Settling them at their desks, I moved back to mine. Sitting down, I observed the other envelope lying there, just calling to be opened. *But not now.* Decision made, I slid it into my purse, willing my curiosity to back off. *Later... when I can focus on it...all by myself.*

* * *

Emily had gone to her fiancé's home for the weekend and had already left by the time I got home from work. I walked in, loaded down with several grocery bags, determined not to make more than one trip from my car. By the time I made it, I was glad to have a first-floor apartment. Dropping everything down on the floor, I was grateful for the upgraded plush carpet to cushion my purchases. Bending to only grab a few at a time now, I carted them into the kitchen.

I put the ice-cream in the freezer, the eggnog in the refrigerator and all the other items away as well. I uncorked the white wine immediately and poured a glass. Licking the semi-sweet riesling off my lips, I stared at my purse, still on the floor by the front door. *His letter is in there.* I couldn't pretend I was not dying to open it, but had managed to wait until school was over, the grocery shopping complete, and now…there was no reason to wait.

Bending over, I pulled the envelope out of my bag and, taking my wine glass to the living room, I perched on the sofa. My eager hands ripped at the envelope, taking out his letter and another picture. His photo fell out face down and I refused to look at it until I read his letter. Placing it on the coffee table next to the wine glass, I opened the paper, my heart pounding for a reason I could not name.

Dear Brooke Thompson,

I hope it's all right that I am writing to you separately. I find that I look forward to the class packages and letters so much, but have to admit that after seeing your picture, it is easier to imagine you as real. I suppose there are things that I can tell you, that I am uncertain about saying to the kids, not knowing how much of war they really can understand. If you consider this inappropriate, please just let me know.

This is my second tour here and I only have seven more months to go. At that time, I'm not sure if I'll re-enlist or not. I guess I'm keeping my options open. I told the kids that I work on helicopters. That's true, but I didn't tell them it was the Apache helicopters. They're armed, attack helicopters, but I don't know if the kids need to know that. They are used in the fighting and are a real advantage in the war. I get to work on the flight controls and cryptography equipment, and perform weapons checks. The work is intense, but it's really interesting.

Sometimes I get bored, but I try to stay busy during my off hours. I was truthful when I told the kids what I do to fill up my time, but will admit to you that sometimes the tedium can drive me crazy. The worst thing is the constant sand and dust that gets blown into everything. We call it

Moon Dust. It's like a tan flour that covers everything. Sometimes I wonder if my lungs are coated with it.

How long have you been a teacher? I can certainly say that I never had a teacher that looks like you, but that's probably a good thing – I might not have graduated if I'd had someone so pretty. I have to admit, it's cool that your school is in Virginia since that is where I'm from. I grew up in Roanoke and my dad still lives there. Are you from Chesapeake?

I don't get a chance to get on the computer very often, but I'm including my email if you want to email me sometime. I also wanted to offer to Skype with the class if you're interested. We'd have to get it set up because of the time difference but we could make it work.

I suppose that is all for now, but I'd love to hear from you sometime, if you would like to correspond. I'll let you filter some of the information to the kids since you know what's best to tell them. I'll close for now but hope you will write back sometime. I'd love to know more about you.

Your friend, Ethan Miller

I ran my finger over the words, Ethan now more real than before. Shifting my eyes over to the coffee table, I leaned up to pick up his picture. Flipping it over, I gasped. Dressed in a tan t-shirt that showed off his thick muscles, and camouflaged pants, he grinned toward the camera. His short, brown hair was slightly longer on top. The crinkles next to his blue eyes showed how much he smiled...or maybe it was from the sun. He was a glorious specimen of a man and I realized just how long it had been since I had had a date...much less a boyfriend. *God, he could get anyone and here I am, drooling over him like some teenager!*

I drained the rest of my wine before leaning back on the sofa. Christmas music played on the TV and I'd plugged in the lights we had strung up around the window.

With Emily gone, I had not put up a tree. Looking around, I realized how lonely my life had become.

I had a great roommate, good friends, and I liked my co-workers. And of course, I loved my students. But something was missing. That spark...the connection with someone else. *And I feel this with Ethan?* Pursing my lips, I shook my head. There is no way I can feel this for someone I have never met other than through letters.

Grabbing my laptop from the end table, I opened up Facebook. I wonder...typing in Ethan Miller, I found quite a few. Biting my lip, I then added U.S. Army into my search. There were still a few, but I quickly found his profile. *I'd recognize those blue eyes anywhere now!* I clicked through his information. Single. *Thank God!* My finger hovered over the Friend Request button for an instant before I clicked.

Glancing back down to his picture, my heart pounded. Running my finger over his features, I smiled. Well, what's the harm in a little infatuation, even if it's one-sided?

That night, lying in bed, my imagination ran wild as I fell asleep, images of a handsome, blue-eyed man, with a heart-stopping smile, invading my dreams.

CHAPTER 5

(JANUARY – ETHAN)

The freezing wind's bite made this place miserable. But, then, so did the summer sun. Maybe it's just a miserable place. Or maybe since I get out in a few months, I'm just sick and tired of being here.

Wearing my winter coat, bundled against the cold, I trudged toward the hangar. The sun was not up, but with a mission eminent, the Apache helicopters needed to be maintained. Hearing the hustle of footsteps, I did not have to turn around to know Jon was pounding the sand behind me.

Catching up with me, we hurried inside, grateful for the chance to get out of the bitter cold. *I wonder what it's like in Virginia right now?* If I were honest with myself, I would have to admit those thoughts entered my mind often...or maybe all the time. What was Brooke doing? How are the kids? Do they talk about me? Does she think about me?

The bustling hangar quickly took my mind off her and back onto the job. We had a lot to do and, from the looks of things, it needed to be done quickly. But nothing could be done half-assed in this work—these birds needed to be able to fully function without any malfunctions.

As Jon and I got to work, a few of the pilots came by, checking on equipment and letting us know of any particular concerns they had. While the hangar was cold, I was grateful to be out of the wind. The winters in Afghanistan were brutal—a fact vividly brought back to mind as soon as I stepped outside once more and was slapped by the icy-cold wind.

By the end of the day, pent-up frustrations had me itching for a physical workout. Entering the tent filled with gym equipment, I shucked off my outerwear, down to my t-shirt and shorts. After a warmup, I began with the free weights, enjoying the burn from the repetitions. The room began to fill as more soldiers finished their duties and I worked my way around the room, using the different equipment.

The banter was light—the camaraderie strong. But I was beginning to want more. More than another tour in the Army. Twenty-four years old and I knew when spring came and my tour was over, I was going home. Home to Virginia. And that thought made me wonder if there was something to go home to.

"Where the fuck is your head?" Burt called out, jolting me out of my musings.

Looking up with what must have been a dumbass expression on my face, he just laughed.

"You've been standing there staring off into space for about five minutes straight." Smirking, he added, "I sure hope whoever she is, you'll share!"

Ignoring his jib, I stalked toward the showers. He was right—my mind was on a girl. But no fuckin' way would I share! The warm water sluiced over my body, washing away the sweat, but did nothing for my raging hard-on. Gripping my cock in my hand, grateful for the private shower stall, I pumped my fist up and down, my mind filled with the image of Brooke. Closing my eyes I could imagine it was her hand…or mouth…working my dick. It did not take long for my body to shudder with the force of my orgasm as I shot cum down into the drain. With one hand on the wall propping my body up, my chest heaved in exertion.

Drying off, I pulled on my clothes once more, adding layers just to get to the DFAC tent for our meal. The wind hit my face as soon as I exited the showers and I jogged the rest of the way, attempting to keep my body warm. Later, entering my tent, I headed straight back through the bunks to mine and saw a large box sitting on my bed.

Jon was standing nearby, grinning, and said, "They let me pick it up for you…I figured you didn't need to go back out into this fuckin' freezin' weather." His gaze dropped down to the box and he licked his lips like a mongrel dog. "Anyway, I figured there might be something good inside that you'd be willing to share with your ol' buddy."

Before I could step closer, he whipped out a knife and, with a grandiose gesture, said, "Here, allow me!" With a flick of his wrist, he slit the box open and stepped back.

Shaking my head in laughter, we both leaned over, peeking inside. I began lifting out books, magazines, toiletries, bags of candy and more homemade cookies. Jon's long arm reached in, snatching the cookies before I had a chance to protest, but since it got him moving out of my way and back over to his bunk, I didn't complain.

Quickly reaching the large envelope, I ripped it open, my heart leaping as I saw not only the one filled with the children's letters but a thick one with Brooke's hand-writing on the outside. *Hell, yeah—Score!*

By now, we were surrounded by other bunkmates, all with their hands out toward Jon and the bag of cookies. "Save me just one, bro," I called out, wanting to make sure I could honestly tell whichever student made the cookies that I had eaten one. He nodded so I went back to the letters.

While Jon dished out the goodies, I leaned against the headboard, my pillow pushed behind my back, and ripped open the kids' notes. Another picture fell out and I flipped it over to see the kids lined up, holding a sign with the words **Come Home Soon** painted across the front. Their innocent smiles faced the camera and my heart warmed at the sight of their familiar faces. I was now able to recognize them by name and personalities.

Chloe was the baker in the group. Chad wanted to be a mechanic and, once he found out I worked on helicopters, he had lots of questions. Sarah was a worrier and constantly asked if I was homesick. I read through their letters, now taking notes so that I could answer their questions.

Dear SPC Miller,

We got snow the other day and got to have a day at home. It doesn't snow too much here, but we watched the weather in your hometown of Roanoke and we saw where their schools got a whole week off because of snow. Do you get snow there? Our teacher said it gets cold where you are. Do you get off work when it snows? Do the heli-copters get to fly in the snow? Love, Todd

Dear SPC Miller,

I hope you like the scarf that is in the package. My

grandma knit it when I told her that we were sending you a package. She said that she prayed for you while she worked on it. She made it out of brown yarn so you can wear it with your uniform. Our teacher said you have to stay in your brownish uniform. If you want, she can make some gloves to match. And she'll pray more if she does.
Love, Sybil

Dear SPC Miller,

I had Miss Thompson show me the Apache helicopters you work on. How cool! Do you think I can fly them when I get older? My dad said that my great-grandpa flew in a war called Vietnam. I don't think that is close to you because I looked it up on our map. I decided to learn everything I could about the helicopters so that if you get to visit us, we can talk about them.
Tyronne

Dear SPC Miller,

I can always tell when one of your letters comes because Miss Thompson gets a special smile on her face. I know she thinks we are all busy writing our letters but I watch her when she reads your letter over again. I like the way it makes her smile. She's always really pretty but I think she gets prettier when she is thinking about you. I hope you can come see us sometime. You would like her and I know she would love to see you in person. Xxoxx
Nicole

All other thoughts fell far away as I read the last letter. *Brooke gets a special smile on her face when she reads my letters?* Closing my eyes for a second, I could imagine her sitting at a desk, her long hair framing her face as her delicate fingers hold the paper and her face beams in the same smile as I've seen in my dreams.

"You okay?" Bill called out as he walked past my bunk.

Jolting, my eyes shot open and I hoped the shadows underneath the bunk kept my blush hidden. "Yeah, sure," I replied.

By now, the gang had gotten a cookie and headed away, leaving just Jon sitting on his bunk staring at me. Lifting an eyebrow, I asked, "What are you staring at?"

Chuckling, he said, "I'm looking at a man who's completely gone for some chick he's never met."

Months ago, I would have called him a liar or cracked a joke, but it died in my throat. *He's right...and how fuckin' crazy is that?* Sighing heavily, I pushed the kids' letters back into the envelope and looked down at the other one—the one that I knew had her letter just for me in it. "Yeah... you're right," I confessed, not meeting his eyes.

"Don't sweat it, man. She writes to you, separate from the kids in her class, so she's got to be feeling something too."

"Or maybe she's just taking pity on me," I bit back, hating the idea.

Shrugging slightly, he stood, tossing the almost empty cookie bag next to me. Stretching, he said, "Doubt it. But you'll never know if you don't keep this little pen-pal thing going. Who knows? Could be your one fuckin' great love." Grinning, he walked away, calling over his shoulder, "Going to play pool. Catch you later."

And with that, I was alone again, staring at the last letter in my hand. Sucking in a deep breath, I let it out slowly as I slid my finger under the flap and opened the missive. A couple of pictures were tucked inside the folds of paper and my heart pounded erratically once more. One was a close-up of Brooke, and I recognized it was her teacher's photograph. The lights caught the golden high-lights in her blonde hair and she wore a headband as the waves of length fell about her shoulders. Her pink mouth, widely smiling, showed off perfect teeth. Her green eyes focused on the camera, but it was easy to imagine them focusing on me. *What would it be like to have that face smiling at me every day?*

The next picture was of her sitting in front of a large stone fireplace, her arms wrapped around her bent legs. Her head was thrown back in laughter and I was sucked into the image. I wanted to be there with her. I wanted her to be laughing with me. I wanted to be the one she stared at when her eyes sparkled. *Damn, Jon is right. I am completely, fuckin' gone for this girl.*

Setting the pictures aside, I unfolded her pages and held my fingers to the words for a few seconds before reading them, attempting to pull her essence from the ink.

Dear Ethan,

I was so glad to get your letter and I am enclosing my email as well. I would love to Skype with you and we can certainly set up a time when the children can see you.

I grew up in the Virginia Beach area, but attended Radford University, which is near Roanoke. That is such a lovely area and I like the mountains too. Is Roanoke where you will go when you get out? Your father must be so proud of you! If you get a chance to come to Chesapeake, please let me know. I would love to meet you in person.

I have an older brother, who is an accountant and lives in Washington D.C. He's engaged to a nurse and they plan to get married next year. My parents still live in the house I grew up in. It was in a nice, but older neighborhood and I still like to visit. The streets are ideal for jogging and they have block parties where all the neighbors will have a cookout together.

I've got a great family, but need my privacy! I live in a two-

bedroom apartment with a roommate, but she is getting married in a few months and so I will be looking for a new roommate. I have friends but don't get out a lot other than work. I really hate to have to try to find someone on Craig's List, but I am getting desperate to find a roommate. The rent isn't too bad if I had to pay it all myself but it would be nice to share the rent with someone. We'll see...I have a few months to find someone.

I've been teaching for two years (yes, I'm 24 years old). I have no idea how old you are, but from your picture I'd guess mid 20's. Am I close? I love the kids and was lucky to get the job I have in the school I wanted. Most teachers hate teaching 4th grade...the kids can be a bit difficult, but I really like this age. They are inquisitive and the world has not taken away their enthusiasm! (but old enough that I don't spend my days wiping noses!)

I'm trying to think of what else to tell you. I'm single. Like I said, I don't get out too much, so you'd probably think I was totally boring! I do run for exercise and have been working up to run in a half-marathon this spring. The naval base holds one here every year.

I hope you are well and staying safe. I confess to thinking of you often and even find myself worrying about you. I now watch the news carefully just to see if I hear of anything happening there that would make me feel closer to you. Anyway, this is all for now, but please write soon. If you want to Skype, we can try it ourselves before trying it with the kids, just to make sure we have the time difference right. Take care!

Love, Brooke

Her words soothed over my heart, still pounding out a rock beat. *Love, Brooke.* I knew it didn't mean anything, but seeing the words made me smile. My gaze skimmed the letter once more, memorizing every detail of her life that she shared. *She must be interested...there's no way she would share so much if she wasn't.* At least as that thought hit me, I hoped I was an object of her interest and not just a project.

I knew something was changing…something had moved inside of me and I was going to see where this new feeling would take me. Locking the letters away in my footlocker, I tucked her pictures on the inside lid with the others and headed back out into the night, jogging straight to the communications tent.

CHAPTER 6

(FEBRUARY – BROOKE)

Elementary classrooms are filled with hearts decorating every surface this time of year, but for single adults, Valentines is a sucky holiday…and makes us think of the love we don't have.

Saturday morning dawned bright with a deep chill in the air and frost on the ground. Dressed warmly, I left the apartment, my morning jog taking me along the park path near my apartment. The cold air sent an ache through my lungs until my body acclimated. I thought of Ethan in the freezing Afghan winter and knew that my discomfort was nothing compared to his.

I did that a lot now…well, almost all the time. No matter what I was doing, I thought of him. It began as wondering what he was doing each day and then slowly morphed into wondering what it would be like if he were here with me. *God, this is such dangerous territory!* I was falling for someone I had never met, but it appeared I was helpless to stop the tidal wave of feelings.

I still longed for the letters that came to the classroom, but now we had advanced to emails. The first time I saw his name in my inbox, I could not contain my scream of excitement. Emily had come running into the room, panicked at my outburst.

Then I had to listen to her incessant questioning about *my soldier,* as she likes to call him. Now, as my feet pounded the sidewalk through the park, I turned those two words over in my mind. *My soldier.* I don't know what Ethan is. A pen-pal? No, that's not enough. A friend? Definitely. Something more? Who knows!

As I rounded a curve, I saw a man in uniform standing near the entrance to the park. The world slowed to a crawl as my feet led me closer and closer. My breath came rushing out much too fast, but I was unable to control the pants. *Could Ethan have gotten out sooner...could he have come to surprise me? Could*—now that I was able to see the man up close I determined it wasn't him. A mixture of embarrassment and disappointment flooded my being and I turned away, feeling foolish tears sliding down my frozen cheeks.

Jogging back to my apartment, I was thankful Emily was gone for the weekend, saving me from having to explain my breakdown. I entered the warmth and walked straight to the refrigerator, taking out a bottle of water. Drinking deeply, I held on to the counter as my rubbery legs regained their strength.

Walking into the bathroom, I stripped out of my running attire and stepped into the hot shower. The water coasted over my body, washing away the sweat and warming me at the same time. Lathering my hair, I then grabbed the shower gel and began running my hands over my body. And wishing Ethan was sharing the shower with me.

Those were the other thoughts that had been creeping in. I wanted to hang onto his broad shoulders as his hands slid over me. I wanted to have his blue eyes peer into mine as we pleasured each other. I knew he was much larger than me. Would shower sex work? Unable to stop the grin, I knew I was more than eager to see if shower sex with him would work!

Climbing out, I toweled off and threw on some comfy, black yoga pants and a baggy, pink sweatshirt. Donning fuzzy pink socks completed my stay-at-home attire. I had nowhere else to go and decided a lazy weekend of binge watching TV shows, cleaning the apartment, and grading some papers would be more than enough to occupy my time.

A few hours later, a ding from my phone alerted me to an incoming email. Unable to hold back the rush of adrenaline at the thought of Ethan, I grabbed my laptop and fired up my email. *Yes! It's him!*

Dear Brooke,

So glad to get your last email. I have to confess it makes my day when I hear from you. How are the kids? You can tell them hi from me and they'll get more letters from me soon. In fact, I've sent a gift to you – it's not much, but I hope you'll like it.

You asked about my dad but we don't talk much. He kind of emotionally disappeared after my mom died, so while we're not estranged, we're just not close. I joined the Army right after high school and have been a soldier for six years, so I don't get back to see him very often. I honestly couldn't tell you if he was proud or not since he really keeps to himself.

It sounds like you've got a great family. I don't know where I'll be going when I get out this spring, but I won't be moving back to Roanoke. With my skills, I can get a job at an airport or even on a naval base. Who knows – maybe I'll check out Chesapeake!

I really loved the pictures you sent. I keep them safe in my footlocker and your face is the last thing I look at before I go to bed and the first thing I look at in the morning. I hope that doesn't creep you out. But when things get bad here, I like to hold onto something nice.

I don't know about you, but I hate winter almost as bad as the summers here. Spring and fall are fairly decent, but right now the cold just penetrates everything. I really can't complain though, because a lot of my work on the helicopters is indoors, so at least I can stay away from the wind while working. We use a lot of computers, so our equipment needs to stay as safe from the elements as possible. The hangars where we work aren't air conditioned or heated, so the weather is still a factor.

I was thinking about you needing a roommate and really hate thinking of you taking someone you don't know. Are you sure there's not someone you know who could use a place to live? Maybe you could check with some of your teacher friends. Trying to find a roommate off Craig's List just seems risky. I know it might seem odd, but I find myself worrying about you.

I'll say Happy Valentine's day, but admit we don't celebrate it here. You probably have a hot date, don't you?

All right, I've got to go, but look for the package soon.

Love, Ethan

Love, Ethan. Just those two words seared through my soul before I shook my head in frustration. Stop acting like you're fourteen, I chastised myself. But I knew it was pointless to try to stop from falling. This man, this soldier, had become important to me. And he was coming back to the United States in three months. Sucking in a deep breath, I thought back over the five months we had been corresponding. *Okay, I can do this...I can wait three more months.* At least I hoped I could.

* * *

Finishing the math lesson for the day, I rang the small bell on my desk, alerting the children that we were moving to a different topic.

"Okay, I wanted to let you know that we are going to be able to Skype with Specialist Miller sometime next week. He and I will try it out this weekend to make sure we can connect."

The students' shouts of glee showed their excitement and I quickly raised my hands to shush them before their exuberance brought the principal down to our room.

"I know you're excited," I grinned. "I am too. And," picking up a large, padded envelope from the floor, I added, "we have more letters!"

Opening the envelope, the children were ecstatic to each receive a short note from Ethan. *Oh, my God! How long did it take him to write all those!* Granted the notes were not long, but each child in the class got one addressed to them.

Reaching into the envelope, my fingers wrapped around something soft. Pulling it out, I discovered an ARMY t-shirt. I could tell it was not brand-new and in fact, when I held it close, the faint scent of after-shave was on it. A note was paper-clipped to the top.

I hope you don't mind that I sent one of my shirts – I promise it's not old! But I have worn it and washed it a couple of times. Can't wait to Skype with you and the kids. Love, Ethan

Nothing in the world could have held back my grin as I

tucked the shirt into my school bag to take home. Still beaming, I had the students put away their notes after they shared. Moving to the next lesson, the children were soon working in small groups as I made my way around the room, checking on their progress. Finally sitting back down at my desk, I pulled out a stack of papers to grade when one of the girls slid up next to me. Assuming she wanted to use the girl's restroom, I reached for the bath- room pass, but her question caught me off guard.

"Are you in love with Specialist Ethan?" Nicole asked, her innocent face full of hope.

No one in the class heard her whispered question and I stammered out my reply. "Wh...what? I don't...I mean...we just—"

"I think it would be nice if you were in love with him. I told him that I thought you might be."

My eyes flew wide open as I realized I had not moni- tored the children's letters. "You told him that?" I squeaked.

Nodding while beaming, she said, "Yep! I told him you always smile when we get packages from him."

Blushing to my roots, I remained silent while nodding for her to take her seat. Stunned that my feelings showed so much on my face, I abandoned the stack of papers on my desk, knowing my concentration was shot for the day.

* * *

The next Saturday morning, I sat nervously waiting next to my laptop. Emily wandered through the dining room, lifting her eyebrow as she looked at my ARMY shirt.

"You wear it to bed every night...are you going to start wearing it every day now?"

"No," I retorted, "but I thought he might like to see it when we Skype today."

Her face brightened instantly as she gushed, "That's today? Ooh, when?"

Glancing at the clock on my laptop, I confessed, "Probably not for another half hour but it could come in at any time. I wanted to be ready."

"Wish I could stay to see the hottie soldier, but I'm heading out." Her eyes shifted to my choice of shirt again and she laughed.

As she walked out, I panicked. I should have worn something cute...or sexy...or—

My laptop alerted that a Skype call was incoming. My heart pounded and my cursor hovered over the accept button as I swallowed audibly. Pressing it quickly before I chickened out, my screen was suddenly filled with Ethan's face. His gorgeous, smiling, blue-eyed face.

Neither of us spoke for a few seconds as we stared at each other. Then we both smiled at the same time and began to speak.

"God, you're gorgeous!" he exclaimed, eliciting a nervous laugh from me. "I know that makes me sound like a prick," he said, shaking his head, "but I thought I was ready to see you and now realize you are so much prettier in person."

My face flamed with pleasure and my only response was to laugh. "Well, if it makes you feel better, I was thinking the same thing about you."

We stared for a moment and I observed his eyes dropping below my face before shooting back up. "You're in my t-shirt," he said, a broad smile breaking across his face.

Deciding not to hide anything, I confessed, "I wear it to sleep ever since I received it. And I thought you might like to see it on me." Hoping my words did not make me sound like a pathetic groupie, I waited to see his response.

His smile deepened as he replied, "Hot damn, Brooke.

Just the image of you in my t-shirt will carry me the rest of the way through my tour."

My shoulders slumped in relief and I was sure my smile matched his. We only had about ten minutes to talk, so I wanted to make the most of our time. We stumbled over our words as we tried to find out all we could, my nervousness overlapping my excitement. The minutes were up way too soon and I bit my lip in anticipation of his goodbye.

His eyes pierced the computer screen at mine, and he said, "Brooke, seeing you makes me want to come home now. And come home to you."

Butterflies took flight in my stomach as I said, "I want you to get home safe and sound. And if that leads you to me, then that would be perfect."

"Really?" he asked. "You really want me to come to you?"

Nodding, I grinned. "I have no idea what's happening here, Ethan, but yes...I want to see you when you get back."

With a nod and a flash of his panty-melting smile, he agreed. "Okay, Brooke...first stop will be Chesapeake. And if I'm lucky...it might be my only stop."

With hasty goodbyes, the computer screen went blank, leaving me to mull over his last words. Leaning back in my chair, I let out a huge sigh. *I have no idea what's happening, but I'm willing to find out!*

My phone rang and I jumped, for a millisecond wondering if it was Ethan. Giving myself a mental shake, I realized he did not have my phone number, wouldn't have just called my phone after Skyping, and I seriously had an Ethan-induced fantasy. Grabbing my cell, I grinned as I saw the caller.

"Hi, mom," I greeted.

"Hey, sweetie," she returned. "I wanted to see if you wanted to have dinner with dad and me soon."

Still grinning, I agreed. "Sure, I'll come next weekend. I've got grades due this week, so my evenings will be filled."

"So anything new going on? Is Emily's wedding plans on schedule?"

"Yeah and I'm happy for her, but sad to lose her as a roommate." Hesitating, I wondered if I should share about Ethan with mom.

Before I had a chance to ponder, she asked, "Is something going on because you sound distracted?"

Deciding to take the plunge, I blurted, "Mom, do you remember the class project of writing to a soldier? Well, we're doing it and we've gotten to know each other a little better."

"Okay," she replied, "but it sounds like there's something else you want to tell me."

"Is it possible to fall for someone you haven't even met?"

The words hung out between us, the silence stretching across the airwaves.

"Are you saying you're falling for this soldier?" she asked, the incredulity ringing loudly in her voice.

"I don't know exactly," I fudged. "I really look forward to his letters. We've Skyped, so I've seen him…just not in person. And I find myself hoping that when his tour is over, he'll come back to Virginia so I can meet him for real. Is that crazy?"

"Oh, honey, I don't think it's crazy at all. But you need to go slow and realize that what you may be experiencing is no more than an infatuation."

"I know…but I'd still like to meet him."

"And I hope you can," she replied. "I truly do. It's been a long time since I've heard you speak positively about any guy and, of course, he has to be on the other side of the world!" Mom laughed and I had to admit it sounded absurd.

Saying our goodbyes, I disconnected before leaning back on the sofa, my hand absently smoothing over the soft cotton ARMY t-shirt. Sighing loudly, I knew it was no use trying to convince myself otherwise...my heart was already involved.

CHAPTER 7

(MARCH – ETHAN)

I was nervous…and hell, I never get nervous!

But I sat at the computer, wiping my sweaty palms on my pants, checking my watch for the zillionth time. Finally, Skype dinged an incoming call and I pressed accept.

There she was—the woman who slid into my life, becoming so important to me. The last time we Skyped, Brooke wore my shirt and rocked my world as we talked.

This time she was prim and proper in her blouse and sweater and oh, so adorable. Who knew I had a secret, sexy-teacher fantasy?

Brooke was grinning at me and then said, "Specialist Miller, Hello and welcome to Eastville Elementary School. I would like to introduce you to the rest of your pen-pals."

She turned the computer camera around and there they were. All twenty-four faces smiling back at me. They were gathered together, some sitting cross-legged on the floor and others kneeling behind them. In the last row, were the tallest children and in the background was a **Come Home Soon, SPC Miller** sign hanging on the wall. *Fuckin' A!*

I heard Brooke's voice in the background give instructions. "Okay, just like we practiced, starting with Chloe, say your name loud and clear so that he can hear you."

The children did exactly what she asked and I grinned at each one, recognizing them from their pictures and letters. I knew which ones always asked about the guns, which ones asked about the weather, and which ones sent cookies. As the last boy called out his name, they then asked a few questions which I knew had been scripted as well.

"Kids, it's great to see you. I've looked at your pictures enough that I think I could have called out your names without you having to tell me. I really like the letters and the goodies you have sent. Yes, it's still very cold here and won't start getting more like spring for another month. I can still see snow on the mountains behind our base. Your teacher has told me that you've been studying hard this year and she is so proud of all of you. I really hope to get to come see you near the end of the school year. Thanks again for taking the time to become my special friends."

After I talked to them as a group, I smiled wider as the camera panned back around to Brooke.

"Well, Ms. Thompson," I said formally, "I'm so glad to meet you and the students today. This has meant a lot to me." The words sounded stiff to my ears but they were true. Those students, as well as their teacher, were crucial to me.

I watched as she blushed and ducked her head. Her smile threatened to turn into a laugh as she replied, "Well, you know this has meant a lot to me too." She held up a small piece of paper, meant only for my eyes and I knew the children could not see it.

It may be crazy, but I miss you. Cannot wait to see you in person. Yours, Brooke

After she had lowered the paper, I had just enough time to say, "Same here," before we had to end the Skype.

Leaning back in my chair, I knew I had a shit-eatin' grin on my face but was unable to wipe it off. A couple more months and I'd have the chance to meet her face to face.

* * *

My footlocker was filling with the letters that came more often now and the emails were becoming a weekly occurrence. Skyping when we could manage was pure heaven. I was no longer falling for Brooke...I was a gone man from the first time I saw her in my ARMY t-shirt. She could not have been more branded as mine than if she had a Property of Ethan tattoo across her chest. And all I wanted to do was pound my own chest in a Neanderthal gesture.

I craved every picture of her and as soon as her image appeared on the computer screen, my heart beat so loudly, I was sure she would be able to hear it. Because of the time difference, we could only Skype privately on weekends that I wasn't on duty, but each time I saw her, it was as though I were seeing her for the very first time.

Her green eyes captivated me, as much as her slightly upturned nose, and rosy-pink lips. And the row of freckles that peppered across her cheeks. There was nothing about this woman that did not turn me on and that included the little snort that would escape when she laughed. No silly, coy giggle for her—nope, my girl had a full on belly-laugh followed by a little snort that made her laugh even more.

She was funny, smart, and gorgeous. I knew her favorite food was shrimp and her favorite color was pink. She watched football but liked baseball more. She thought about getting her master's degree as a reading specialist but hadn't decided to go back to school yet. And as of now…she still did not have a roommate for when Emily got married. Sitting back, I glowered at the thought of her just taking anyone to help with rent.

"What the fuck's got you looking like you want to kick the shit outta someone?" Jon asked, observing me from his side of the Apache.

"I was just thinking about Brooke," I answered.

"Something wrong in paradise?"

"She needs a new roommate this summer and is looking on Craig's list for a replacement. That just doesn't sound very secure to me."

"So why don't you apply for the position?" Jon asked. Still smirking, he said, "'Cause let's be honest. You've got lots of positions you'd like to be in with her!"

"God, your jokes are getting worse," I complained, but secretly admitted he was right. The thought of being in any position with Brooke had the effect of getting me rock hard instantly. Forcing my mind to something else, our banter was interrupted by our Sergeant. "Miller. Bolten. Meeting in the Captains's office. Now."

Sharing a look of surprise, we jumped up and immediately fell in behind our Sergeant as we headed down the hall to a row of offices. Once inside, we met up with two other members of our squad. The meeting was quick and to the point. We were being temporarily re-assigned to a smaller base, higher in the mountains. It was being used to land some of the Apache helicopters and they needed mechanics. We were told we were picked because the Sergeant claimed we were the best. A nice compliment, but coming near the end of my tour was not exactly welcome.

Walking out thirty minutes later, the four of us headed back to our tent to prepare for the re-assignment. We had two hours to pack up and get our gear to the helicopter port. We'd be transported by an old MI-8 helicopter to the new base. Helicopter flying was not my favorite mode of transportation, even knowing we'd have armed coverage. Rubbing the back of my neck, I cleared my mind focusing on the tasks at hand.

Jon looked over at me and said, "Damn, man. You only had two more months to go. At least this assignment is temporary. Sarge said four weeks at the most."

"It's all good," I replied, my mind already wrapping around the duty. Opening my footlocker, I halted at the pictures inside. Several of the class and a growing number of photographs of Brooke. Beautiful Brooke. Throwing my things inside, I called out, "Gotta get to the communication tent and send an email to Brooke to let her know I'll be out of contact for a month."

Taking off at a run, I pounded down the dusty lane, quickly throwing open the door and rushing inside. Another soldier was just finishing, and I shouted for him to not disconnect. Sliding into his now empty seat with hasty thanks, I fired off an email to Brooke. As I hurried back to the bunk, I knew it would be the longest month of my life.

* * *

Two weeks later, I pushed open the tent flap, closing it quickly behind me. Exhaustion pulled at my body as I crawled onto my cot, fully dressed. I'd eaten a quick meal before heading to my tent, knowing once I landed on my cot I would not want to get back up.

The work was steady as the birds flew mission after mission and we were responsible for making sure they were working and armed.

The Apaches required constant servicing and arming,

both duties taking a toll on those of us working in shifts around the clock. The fighting had intensified and I had to admit, the war felt real up here. Back on the main base, it was easy to forget that the war was raging around us when we were insulated. While I knew danger lurked, I always felt safe there.

But here? Jesus, the war was much closer...too close to be honest. I knew the pilots were tired...hell, we all were. But no one complained. There was a job to do and we all did it.

The base was tiny compared to where we had been and I'd give my paycheck for a good cup of hot coffee. Or a really hot shower. But what I really missed were the letters. I wanted to see Brooke's now familiar handwriting on the envelope and hear more about her life. Hell, I wanted to read the notes from the kids. Somehow in just a few months, they had all become important to me. Yeah...I'd definitely give my paycheck for a letter to give me a mental break from this hell-hole.

Our tent only held four Army cots and the back of it was pressed up against the sides of the tunnel partially dug in the mountainside. Stacked sandbags lined the front and sides, providing little relief from the cold, but would hopefully keep stray bullets from penetrating.

The cold seeped in more than before and we slept fully clothed just to stay warm. Rolling to my side, I leaned my arm out and flipped open my locker. That was how I wanted to go to sleep...with Brooke's face smiling straight at me. I had read and re-read the kids' letters, finding that I missed hearing about them.

Jon staggered in as well, flopping onto his cot, the groans of the wooden slats meeting the groans coming from his mouth.

"Only two more weeks to go," I said, but wasn't sure he

heard me. He began snoring almost instantly. Looking at Brooke's picture one last time before I went to sleep, I reached out and touched her smiling face, anxious for the time when I could touch her skin for real.

* * *

A week later, the sounds of yelling jarred me awake and I sat up quickly, throwing my legs over the side of the cot just as Jon did the same. An explosion close by had us jumping up and grabbing our helmets. Racing from the tent, I looked down the path to where the birds were lined up, pilots climbing aboard.

"Jesus Christ, they've got missiles!" Jon screamed as we watched an explosion rock the earth not far from one of the Apaches.

How the hell the Taliban managed to get a rocket this close to the base I had no idea, but there was no time to think of anything other than to get to where we were needed.

We heard the familiar roar of the main rotors and turboshaft engines as the pilots readied the birds to take off. The Apaches flying out meant that they would need immediate maintenance and re-arming when they returned.

Our boots pounded the path when another whistling missile sounded. Refusing to stop to see where it landed, we kept running. The explosion hit close by, the side of the mountain spewing out in all directions. Throwing ourselves to the ground, we protected our bodies as best as we could until the earth stopped shaking. I could hear the sound of people yelling to stay down, but I had a job to do. Leaping to my feet, I continued to race toward the airfield.

Two of the birds had taken off and I knew within

minutes the threat would be taken care of—the Taliban fire would be as extinct as the men doing the firing. Rounding the back of one of the Apaches, furthest from the others, I saw the pilot climbing in and ran over.

One more incoming missile sounded, this time hitting too close to the Apache next to me. As pieces of it flew apart in the explosion, my world went black.

* * *

Beeping. Fuzzy voices. "Specialist Miller. Ethan. Can you hear me?"

Who's Miller? I floated along, remembering one summer when some buddies and I inner-tubed down a lazy river near our hometown. Weightless, boneless.

Alarms sounding. *Can't someone turn them off?* I opened my eyes but was unable to focus on anything. A dark-haired woman stood next to me, her smile seemed wrong. *Shouldn't she have blonde hair?* Confusion set in as I tried to think of why her hair color mattered.

She reached out and touched my brow before turning back to the beeping monitors. I wanted to tell her to make them quiet, but my mouth did not work.

"Specialist Miller? We're taking off now. We'll see to your comfort and let us know what you need."

I need to sleep. People sound so far away. I must be underwater. That's right – I was floating and must have my head underwater. The river is so peaceful. I think I'll stay here.

* * *

I awoke in Germany. Or, to be exact, a military hospital in Germany. I felt no pain, but then, I felt almost nothing. It took a while for me to figure out who I was, where I was, or remember what happened, but when I did, the first thing I did was jerk my gaze down over my body. Two arms. Two legs. Lifting one hand to my head, I noted it was still intact and with the other hand lifting the sheet, I saw my dick. *Okay...all present and accounted for.*

My left leg was fucked up though and the thought slammed into me that I might not get to keep it. Metal pins stuck out of it and encircled the entire leg from thigh to ankle. I felt no pain in my leg, but then I realized I couldn't feel my leg at all.

My mouth felt stuffed with cotton and the goddamn beeping was still present. Fumbling around underneath the sheet, I found the nurse's buzzer and pressed it continually. In just a moment one arrived, her smile appearing genuine to my distraught mind.

"Specialist Miller, it's good to see you awake—"

"My leg...what's happening to my leg?" I croaked, not recognizing my hoarse voice.

She moved to the side of the bed and picked up a cup of water with a straw. "Here, sip."

I wanted to refuse, but the desire to quench my dry throat won out and I gulped the water. She pulled it away just as nausea hit.

"I said sip for a reason," she softly chided. "You're on a morphine drip to control pain and it can make you nauseous. I'll have the doctor send an order for anti-nausea meds."

I was stuck in bed, unable to move, my chest heaving from the exertion of just sipping the water. Closing my eyes, willing the room to stop swaying, I asked again, "My leg. What's going on with my leg?"

"I'll get the surgeon," and before I could stop her, she left the room. I dozed for an indeterminate amount of time, but the next time I awoke, the surgeon was examining my leg. The medical jargon he spouted did nothing to alleviate my concern, but the most important news he gave indicated they had been successful in saving my life and my leg. *Thank God, they saved my fuckin' leg!* Nothing else he said after that mattered as I drifted back to sleep.

This time my dreams of floating continued, but now they were invaded by images of a beautiful blonde with green eyes standing on the shore waving as I drifted on by, unable to stop.

CHAPTER 8

(APRIL – BROOKE)

My energy for teaching was at an all-time low.

I sat watching the children work on their science homework, knowing state assessments were in less than a month and all I wanted to do was lay in bed. The kids missed getting a letter from Ethan this month even though I explained that he had sent me an email weeks ago, letting me know he was going to be out of communication—whatever that meant! All I knew was that he was going to be away from mail or email for weeks.

Sighing, I looked up at the large clock on the wall and rang the bell on my desk. Time for them to go to music class. As the last child walked out of our room, following the music teacher, I leaned back in my seat, closing my eyes.

I missed Ethan. There was no other reason for my general malaise. I wasn't sick...just heartsick. I could no longer pretend that my feelings for him were just platonic...nope, I was in love and had never met him in person!

I stared at his picture every night before I went to bed,

always sleeping in his t-shirt. It no longer smelled like him, having been washed a dozen times but the super-soft material clung to me in my dreams making me feel closer to him.

Opening my eyes, I spied the large calendar by the classroom door and knew that today marked a month since he had sent the email. Maybe...just maybe, he'll get back in touch this week.

Emily's wedding was a week away and I needed to pull myself out of my slump. *Ethan is working...doing what he needs to do and I've got to get a grip!* Sucking in a deep breath while standing, I walked down the hall to retrieve my class. Greeting them at the door of the music room, I smiled as they lined up.

"Did we get a letter from Specialist Miller?" Nicole asked, her eyes wide and hopeful. "You're smiling!"

My face fell as I realized how much the kids had picked up on my mood. "Oh, I'm so sorry, but no. He's still out of touch." I watched their smiles droop as well and as we entered the room, I clapped my hands together. "Come on, everyone. We have lots to do to keep us active." Drawing them into a history game, I was determined to hide my blue mood from my students.

* * *

A week later, I still had not heard from Ethan. And what was worse was not having any idea what had happened nor having a way to find out. I had sent emails, assuming he would get them when he was able to be back in contact. But no replies. He had mentioned one friend named Jon but, with no last name, I had no one else to try to contact.

Sitting on my sofa with my legs curled up underneath me, I poured over his Facebook page, wondering if there was anyone I could contact. But then a thought began to slither through my mind...*what if he's avoiding me?* Biting my fingernail, I battled this notion, not wanting to consider that perhaps he realized how close he was to getting out of the Army and coming to see me was no longer something he wanted to do.

The front door opened and Emily entered, followed by Chris, her fiancé. Looking over at me, she grinned until she saw me curled in on myself in the corner of the sofa.

"Oh, Brooke, no word yet?"

Forcing a smile on my face, I shook my head, attempting a carefree expression. I think I may have failed. Clearing my throat, I tried to change the subject. "Are you guys moving some things out today?"

Emily walked over and sat on the coffee table, taking my hands in hers. "Yeah," she said softly, her eyes searching mine. "But I feel bad, because I know this is hard on you."

"Oh, my goodness," I exclaimed, squeezing her hands in return. "Do not feel bad! I'm fine. Absolutely fine." Looking over to Chris, I smiled, adding, "You two have lots to be excited about and I, for one, am extremely thrilled about your upcoming wedding!"

I watched as Emily and Chris shared a smile, glad for her that she had found someone to share her life with. "So, what do you need help with?" I asked, hopping up from the sofa.

Most of the furniture was mine, so it did not take long to get Emily's belongings loaded into Chris' truck. Standing on the sidewalk, I hugged both of them. As Chris hopped into the driver's seat, I walked Emily around to the other side. With one last hug, I promised to see her in a week at the rehearsal dinner.

I waved as they drove away before turning to walk back into my apartment...all alone. Plopping down on the sofa, I began to wallow in self-pity and doubt. *Who am I kidding? What kind of a relationship do I really have with Ethan?*

Being alone isn't always bad, but being lonely hurt. I wanted someone to share my life with. Someone to share my ups and downs, good times and difficult ones. And even though he was on the other side of the world, Ethan was beginning to fill that role. *Are we at the beginning of something wonderful or am I pinning my hopes on an impossible dream?* My empty apartment offered no words of comfort.

* * *

The students were once more bouncing off the wall since spring break would begin at the end of this school day. My mind was filled with all that I had to get done, so I knew I was as distracted as the children. As soon as they leave, I have to hurry home to get ready for Emily's rehearsal dinner, then be a bridesmaid in tomorrow's wedding, and then finally have a week off to enjoy.

With only thirty minutes left before the buses came, I rang for the students to gather in their semi-circle. "Okay, everyone. Let's talk about what you plan on doing with a whole week out of school."

Hands shot toward the sky, as each child anxiously wanted to share. Plans for beach trips, visits to grandparents, vacations to Disney World, and even a cruise filled the air.

"What about you, Miss Thompson?" one of the students asked.

Smiling, I replied, "Well, it probably won't sound like fun to you, but my best friend and roommate is getting married tomorrow, so I'll be in the wedding as a bridesmaid and get to have fun at the reception, which is like a big party."

"Oooh, do you get to wear a pretty dress?" Chloe asked.

"Yes," I nodded. "And I'll get to dance and eat good food, including wedding cake."

"I wanted Specialist Miller to come visit and then you two could get married," Nicole said, her mouth in a pout.

I hid my disappointment behind a forced chuckle. "Oh, sweetie, Specialist Miller and I were just friends."

"Were? You're not anymore?" Chad piped up, astute as ever.

"Oh, I mean, *are*...we *are* friends," I corrected, making sure to emphasize the present. Sucking in a ragged breath, I was thrilled when the end-of-day bell rang. The students raced to their desks, grabbing whatever they needed and filed out the door. I stood with a group of teachers on the sidewalk, waving as the buses drove away, just as eager for spring break as the children were.

* * *

Just a little more than twenty-four hours later, I had finished the reception dinner, given my bride and groom toast, and danced with just about every eligible bachelor at the wedding. Finally, taking a break, I found a table near the corner of the reception hall and plopped down in a chair wearily. My last dance partner had complimented how my light green bridesmaid dress made my eyes even more beautiful and all I could think about was Ethan when he told me how much he loved my eyes. Smoothing my hands over the silk material, knowing the dress was perfect for my curves, I realized that not one partner had sparked any interest in me at all. I looked at each one and found him lacking when compared to a tall, broad-shouldered, muscular soldier with sky-blue eyes.

Sighing, I cast my view over the dance floor and

watched as Emily and Chris moved slowly together, their arms wrapped around each other, completely oblivious to everyone else in the room. Smiling at their tangible love, I took another sip of champagne from the flutes being offered by the roving wait staff.

As the song ended, the DJ announced it was time to send off the bride and groom. The assembly gathered along the walkway leading to the limousine, and I had to push my way to the front to make sure I saw them off. Emily rushed over to give me one last hug before being swept away by Chris. As I watched them drive away, my breath caught in my throat as a single tear escaped. Life was changing, but I felt no joy…only emptiness.

* * *

It was almost one o'clock in the morning when the taxi dropped me off at my apartment, slightly tipsy from too much champagne. As soon as I made it through the door, I bent over and slipped off my sky-high heels. Moaning as my bare feet dug into the carpet, I wiggled my toes, working out the kinks.

Smiling at the memory of the beautiful wedding, I looked around at the décor that was now all my own. *Tomorrow I need to continue my search for finding a roommate!*

Walking over to my laptop sitting on the coffee table, I decided that since I wasn't sleepy, there was no time like the present to see if anyone had answered my ad for a roommate. Opening my laptop, I leaned back against the cushions, propping my feet on the sofa next to me. Checking my emails, I scrolled through the spam, the ads, the bills, and…*huh?* There was one from someone named Jon with a military email address. *Jon? Ethan's friend?*

With my heart drumming in my chest, I clicked on his name.

Brooke Thompson,

I have been trying to find the correct Brooke that is a friend of SPC Ethan Miller of the U.S. Army. I did not have your contact information but found an old envelope with the Eastville Elementary school return address and searched you down from that. I needed to let you know that Ethan was injured about five weeks ago while we were on duty. He was sent to Germany for surgery and is now at Walter Reed Medical Center in Maryland. I have not spoken to him, but know that he would want you to know.

SPC Jon Bolten

Injured? Oh, Jesus, Jon doesn't say how badly Ethan was hurt! Jumping up quickly, I paced the floor, chest heaving, trying to think of what to do. Dragging my hand through my hair, tearing at the pins holding it in the ridiculous bridesmaid hairdo, I continued to stalk about the room, my heart pounding.

Think...think! What can I do? Making up my mind, I grabbed my laptop again and began searching.

CHAPTER 9

(MAY – ETHAN)

The ceiling was boring. Utterly, fucking, boring.

And I should know—I've been staring at it on and off for two weeks. Between the hospital in Germany where they saved my leg to Walter Reed Medical Center, where more surgery pinned me all together, I'd seen a lot of the ceilings. Flat on my back, unable to move.

My left leg was still in traction for part of each day. Scars ran from my ankle up to my thigh...*but at least I still have a leg*. As I have looked around the ward, there are many here who don't.

I scrubbed my hand over my face, feeling the need for a shave but, then, it hardly mattered. *No one here to impress.* That thought brought Brooke to the forefront of my mind —not that she was ever far from it. I was so close to having it all. My discharge this month, finally going to meet her, finding a new job...one that was going to keep me close to her, and taking our relationship to the next level. *Hell, I was going to claim her as my own. That next level was going to be staying together forever.* Sighing, I stared at the ceiling some more. What else was there to do?

"Good morning, Ethan," the nurse greeted as she came in to check my vitals.

Forcing a tight-lipped smile to my face, I nodded. "So what's on the agenda today? More ceiling staring?"

Chuckling, she shook her head. "Actually, no. Today, the doctor has ordered for you to get up and get moving."

With a lifted eyebrow, I shot a sardonic look toward her. "Yep, I'm ready for the dance floor right now."

"You can fuss all you want, but at least you won't be staring at the ceiling," she quipped.

It took all my control to not tell her to get the hell out of my room. As much as I wanted to move around more, I knew movement was going to hurt like a fucker and hated the idea of more pain. *Yeah, I'm a wuss, but not everyone wants to jump into the no pain, no gain part of their rehab.* Blowing out a long breath, I knew I had no choice. I had to get my mobility back if I was ever going to accomplish any of the things I wanted to do when I was discharged.

The thought of Brooke once more floated through my mind. *I wonder what she's thinking?* For the first week after I was injured, I was drugged and out of my mind, barely registering the stay in Germany or the medical transport back to the States. Then another week passed as I dealt with more surgery and pain management. And now another week later? I miss her...want her...but refuse to pull her into this mess of mine. I refuse to burden her with what has happened to me.

Just as I was ready to fall down the rabbit-hole of feeling sorry for myself once more, the physical therapist came in.

"Good news, my man," Terrance called out, his wide smile showing off his gleaming white teeth against his dark skin. He clapped his hands then rubbed them together in eager anticipation of my torture.

"You are too fuckin' glad to see me in agony," I groused.

"Aw, come on, Miller. We gotta get you up and about, so you can get your dancin' feet going."

The idea of dancing—or rather not dancing—with Brooke shot my already bad mood to hell. I had wanted to come home and sweep her off her feet. Now looking down at my scarred, pinned leg, I knew my dancing days were over. I knew it was selfish, but right now, any enthusiasm was gone.

"Got no plans on dancing," I retorted, knowing I was being an asshole but seemingly unable to help myself.

"I've seen that picture taped to the side of your bed. Bro, that's one beautiful woman. You can't tell me that she doesn't want you back on your feet."

Not wanting to talk about Brooke, my mouth had a mind of its own when I heard myself say, "She's got no idea anything happened to me."

No words came back at me and I attempted to not look at Terrance until finally I could not stand it. My gaze lifted and observed his hard face—no pity coming from him at all.

"I know what you're going to say," I bit out. Seeing his head tilt to the side, I plunged on. "You're going to tell me that I'm lucky...I was getting out anyway...I've still got my leg...all of those things I already know."

"So tell me something I don't know," he said, his calm voice soothing my ruffled edges.

Sucking in a deep breath, I shook my head for a moment, not knowing how to explain the random thoughts shooting through my head. Finally, realizing he wasn't going to move until I spoke, I said, "We've never actually met in person. Just letters, emails, Skype. But I fell...Jesus, Christ...I fell hard." Another shudder ran through me as I drew a ragged breath. "But I had a plan.

Get out this month...go to see her...sweep her off her feet...and ride off into the fuckin' sunset, I guess."

"From where I'm standing, that plan doesn't seem too impossible."

Shooting him a glare, I retorted, "Yeah, well, you're *standing*."

"And you will be too," he shot back.

"She and I...we haven't had a chance to actually build anything real...not yet. How the fuck am I supposed to dump this on her? I can't walk, not for a while. I sure as hell can't get a job in an airport until I'm fully well. So I've got nothing to offer."

Shrugging as he moved over to release the traction, he said, "Well, if you don't think she's worth the effort, I guess you know best."

A curse was on my lips but fell away as a flash of pain shot through me as Terrance moved my leg. *Jesus, I'm fucked.*

Three hours later I wondered if death would not have been preferable. The torturous pain from being moved up and down, in and out of a wheelchair, attempting to stand without putting any pressure on my leg...this made basic training seem like a proverbial walk in the park. Sweating, cussing, and *if I'm honest*...even crying.

* * *

A week later, my world had devolved into eating, sleep, and rehab. Painful, fuckin' rehab. I had the physical therapy room memorized...each area of torture. I started out on the low, padded wooden table where Terrance moved and bent my leg in what should be normal positions but felt like he was re-breaking the bones. Then I moved to the parallel bars where I practiced pulling myself out of the wheelchair and moving without putting any pressure on my leg. Yeah, right.

I had to do arm workouts to make sure my arms were strong enough to maneuver the wheelchair and leg work-outs for the good leg to make sure it didn't atrophy along with the injured one. All this while staring at the mess of pins and bolts in my leg.

Sometimes I'd stare at the ones who had no leg and know I was an asshole for being pissed about my mangled one, but fuckin' hell…this was not how I wanted my Army career to end.

And right now, the minutes just before dawn, are when my thoughts turned inward and ugly. I know I'm making progress. I hear the words of encouragement from the doctors, nurses, physical therapists. Hell, even from the other patients. And sometimes I feel it too…and other times, like just now as the sun rises, I think of her and grit my teeth in frustration.

It's been weeks since the explosion…add the weeks before that when I was at the temporary assignment, and I feel each of the fifty days since I last had communication with Brooke. There's a computer right down the hall…so close…so easy. *So what the fuck is holding me back?* Everything. Everything I wanted to be for her and everything I'm not.

I'm so afraid to pull up my email. I know she would have written at first—emails full of what the kids were doing, what they were learning, and probably more pictures. It fuckin' hurt knowing their school year would be over in a few weeks and I would not get to see them in person. Brooke and I had it all planned. When I got discharged, I'd go to Chesapeake and just walk into the classroom and watch the kids' excitement. Now, just like everything else, that's all gone down the fuckin' drain.

And what about when she starts wondering why I haven't emailed back? Did she get pissed? Give up? Rubbing the back of my neck where a tension headache was building, I considered finally manning up and checking my email. *God, when did I become such a pussy?*

I looked at the clock and realized it was time for breakfast. *Maybe food will fortify me enough to gain my courage.* I rolled myself down the hall toward the cafeteria. That was one thing I learned quickly here—they start working towards independence as soon as possible. So my special wheelchair that has my left leg sticking straight out was no reason for not getting around. *But then, they've never bumped a pinned leg on the side of an elevator or into someone and felt the pain explode from the toes up. Nope...that would just be me.*

I managed to make it through the food line, getting my chow without spilling anything, setting my tray on my lap so I could roll over to a table. I looked around and saw the walking and rolling wounded. *I'm so much better off than many of these guys, and yet, I feel so pissed.* I had found out that the only two people injured in the attack were the pilot and me and, while I'm grateful Jon escaped, I never got to say goodbye to my squad.

I watched as the Marine next to me struggled with his milk carton. His right hand was missing a few fingers, along with the missing right leg. I reached over and quietly opened the carton, sticking a straw in before handing it back.

I avoided eye contact but heard the "appreciate it, man," from him. With a nod, we ate while beginning to talk haltingly with the others at the table. *Seems like I'm not the only one pissed about the outcome of the war.* Rolling away from the cafeteria, I felt strangely encouraged to make my way to the computer room. I wondered if it would last.

There was no way my straight-legged wheelchair was going to make it under the desk, but I managed to wheel sideways and lean over to punch in my email ID. After wrestling with it, I looked over and realized there were laptops on a table by the window. *Well, fuck, that would have been easier.* Before I decide to try them out, my email pinged up. I had over two hundred new emails.

Not taking the time to delete the ones not needed, I saw Brooke Thompson's name on at least twenty of them. My finger hovered over the key and it did not escape my notice that it was shaking. Breaking out in a sweat, I placed my hand back in my lap. *What am I doing? I can't walk on my own right now...I can't work.* This was not how I wanted her to remember me. And I sure as hell didn't want a pity send-off.

Shutting the computer down, I rolled back to my room.

CHAPTER 10

(MAY - BROOKE)

What a maze! Can this building be any more confusing?

I finally made it inside the section of the Walter Reed Medical Center where I was told Ethan would be. As soon as I had read the email from Jon, I began planning. The WRMC website had been helpful, but not being related to Ethan did not make things easy. He had not listed any restrictions on his visitor list, which worked for me since he had not been able to respond to any of my emails.

Now it was Monday afternoon and after driving for a few hours, I was finally here. Licking my lips nervously, I waited for a visitor's badge and directions to the commons garden.

Walking out into the spring sunshine again, I blinked at the bright light as I viewed the beautiful gardens. Patients walked or wheeled around and I observed many with children running around their parents. Sucking in a fortifying breath, I let it out slowly. My eyes roved over the numerous recuperating servicemen and women, and the idea that I might not recognize him—or be a welcome guest—struck me.

Slowly walking along the sidewalk, I smiled and nodded as I made my way around the gardens. Looking to the left, I saw a man sitting in a wheelchair in the shade underneath a large tree. He was wearing a dark green t-shirt and gym shorts. His hair was longer on top, but still fairly closely cut on the sides. His left leg was supported straight out in front of him. He was looking down at his lap and, as I approached, I noticed him holding a book. There was no doubt—it was Ethan. *I'd know him anywhere.* Heart pounding, I stepped closer, fear and longing warring inside as all the greetings I had practiced now failed me.

* * *

(Ethan)

I had been reading for almost an hour and the warm sun was lulling me to sleep. The sound of children laughing and families enjoying the spring day was nice to see, even if it made me feel more alone. Sighing loudly, I closed my book, deciding it was time to go back inside. A slight noise to my right sent my gaze looking over.

A blonde woman was standing in the shade staring at me, but it took a few seconds for my vision to focus on her face. Blinking several times, I shook my head as though the image in front of me was concocted by my imagination.

My chest heaved as my heart pounded. *Brooke?* The woman stepped closer as she nodded and I realized I had spoken her name aloud.

My eyes never left hers as she approached my chair and knelt next to me. She laid her hand on mine and my breath left my body in a whoosh. "How…?"

"I got an email from Jon. He had problems finding me until he remembered Eastville Elementary." Brooke sucked her lips in as her eyes were pinned on our joined hands. I gently rubbed my thumb over her palm.

Lifting my eyes, I drank her in. She was more beautiful in person than her photos or image had exposed. I had spent so many months thinking of what I would say to her when I first met her, but now the words choked. I watched her bite her lip and recognized her nervous habit. Before thinking, I reached out and rubbed my thumb over her bottom lip, soothing it.

Her green eyes pinned me as she whispered, "Is it okay that I'm here? I...I never heard..."

She let her insecurity and doubt fall between us, tangible in her nervousness. Shame hit my gut and I winced as my hand squeezed hers tighter.

"Oh, Brooke, I'm sorry...I...I didn't know what to do..." My voice trailed off as I broke eye contact, my gaze moving down to my leg.

She reached over, cupping my stubbled jaw with her hand. "Hey, you don't have to explain," she said, dropping her gaze. "I probably shouldn't have just dropped in, but...I wanted to see you so much." Sighing, she cried, "Oh, none of this is coming out the way I envisioned!"

"Hey, hey," I comforted, leaning my face into her palm for an instant, allowing the warmth of her touch to sear me. "Look, this isn't the way I wanted our meeting to be either." Seeing her attention back on me, I continued. "I had it all planned out...the way we were going to meet and, believe me, this was not it."

She shifted her gaze down toward my leg before holding focus on my face. "Can you tell me anything about what happened?"

"That's a tale for another time," I replied, not wanting

our first visit to be any more awkward than it was. "Suffice it to say, I won't be asking you to dance anytime soon." I heard the harshness in my voice but found it hard to control. Ashamed, I dropped my gaze once more.

A chuckle escaped from her lips, as she said, "I can't dance worth a damn anyway, so that won't bother me!"

I looked up at her smiling face and grinned in return. Just then a slight snort escaped, which only caused her to laugh harder. *God, her laughter is better than I imagined!* Unable to stop, I erupted in laughter as well for the first time in a month.

As our mirth slowed, I realized she had been awkwardly kneeling the whole time. "Fuck, your legs must be killing you, squatting like that—" I said, looking around for a seat.

"Thought you two might like this!" a deep voice called out from behind.

Twisting around, I watched Terrance walk over with a folding chair in his arms. Stopping at the wheelchair, he said, "Miss, I gotta tell you, I haven't seen this grumpy bugger laugh since he's been here, so you, my dear, are a miracle worker!"

Smiling, Brooke took the offered seat as I introduced her to my physical therapist. As Terrance turned to leave, he shot me a thumb's up sign as he winked at Brooke.

Laughing again, she hid her mouth behind her hand.

"Don't hide your beautiful smile," I begged, pulling her hand down. "I've wanted to see your face for so long, I don't want to miss anything."

"I tend to laugh too loud and then I snort," she admitted, blushing.

"It's adorable," I said, my eyes once more raking over her face before sliding over the rest of her. Wearing a light blue sundress with little flowers embroidered across the bust drew my eyes to her chest. My cock stirred for the first time in a while and it was hard to hide the relief that my parts were still working.

"Ethan?" she said, her voice caressing his ears. Biting her bottom lip again, she sucked in a deep breath. "What happens now?"

I searched her face, unsure what she was asking. "About...?" I prompted.

Ducking her head, she replied, "About you...and us." Lifting her head to peer into my eyes, she continued, "I hated not being in contact with you and confess that I began to think that perhaps you had decided that you were no longer interested in me." Seeing me about to protest, she squeezed my hand and quickly said, "I just got the email from Jon a week ago and spent a week trying to figure out how to get to you here. At first they wouldn't tell me anything...I didn't even know if you were still here. If I'd known earlier, I would have been right here by your side."

Sighing heavily, I said, "And you're wondering why I didn't contact you." Watching her nod slowly, my heart aching at her pain. "At first, I was on duty and unable to communicate with you. Then...well, after I was injured, I was unable to do anything because I was drugged out of my mind to control the pain and then...," I dragged my free hand through my hair as I admitted, "I was just pissed at the world."

"At me?"

"No, no, never at you. It has only been the last week or so that I was even able to consider checking my emails and all I could think about was how I couldn't be what I wanted to be for you."

She cocked her head to the side. Stroking my hand with her fingers, she waited for me to continue.

"I had this whole thing planned in my head," I confessed, "and it involved sweeping you off your feet." Giving a rueful chuckle, I said, "I guess I've spent too much time feeling sorry for myself." Leaning forward, my hand caressing her cheek. "But seeing you here today has only solidified my resolve to get back to walking as soon as I can."

I leaned the rest of the way in and sealed her lips with mine. Warm and silky, tasting like strawberries, I closed my eyes and breathed her in as my lips continued to explore her mouth. Finally pulling back, breathless, we shared a smile.

"How long do you have to stay here?" Brooke asked, glancing back down to his leg.

"Probably another week or so," I replied. "From what they tell me, I just have to get steady on my feet and then can transition to another facility. The military calls them WTUs for Warrior Transition Units. That's where I'll finish my rehabilitation and transfer to veteran status since I'll be discharged in about three weeks."

"Oh…" she said, disappointment in her voice. "Where will you go?"

Shrugging, I admitted. "I haven't told them where I should be sent, since there's nothing for me where my old man is." I hesitated before admitting, "I did check…there's one at Ft. Eustis in Newport News."

Brooke's green eyes lit as she beamed her smile at me. "That's not far from Chesapeake!"

"Even when I hated what happened, I couldn't get you out of my mind," I grinned. "So, you wouldn't mind me being closer for my rehab?"

"Are you kidding?" she shrieked, leaning forward to cup my cheeks with both hands. "All I want is for you to get better and be as close to me as possible!"

Kissing me again, she gave a slight moan and I took advantage, slipping my tongue inside her mouth. I cursed not being able to take her into my arms, owning the kiss and her body the way I wanted, but with her sweet mouth, she tamed my frustration.

Finally pulling back, she sucked in her lips, blushing. "I didn't mean to come here and do...um...this."

"Doing *this*," I grinned, "is all I've thought about." With both of our hands cupping each other's cheeks, I pulled her forward and kissed her nose. Seeing her wide-eyed surprise, I chuckled. "I've wanted to kiss your nose since I first saw your freckles."

Laughing, Brooke admitted, "I've always hated them but right now, I think maybe I'll stop trying to cover them up!"

The afternoon sun had slid behind the tall buildings and evening shadows were creeping across the lawn. We looked around, noticing most families had made their way inside. Standing, she said reluctantly, "I suppose I should go."

My heart beat against my ribcage as I held on to her hand tightly. "Will you come back?"

Her smile beamed down upon me, chasing away my fear. "Yes, of course. I'll come back as often as I can." Her brow crinkled in thought as she said, "I...could stay in a hotel tonight and come back to see you tomorr—"

"Yes, yes!"

Nodding, she said, "Can I push you in now...or um...do you want to do it yourself?" Appearing nervous, I knew she had no idea how to assist me without pain or insult.

"I like doing it myself, but I've got no problem having you help me get over the grass until we get to the sidewalk."

Moving behind me, she took the brakes off and pushed

me toward the building as I noticed the sunset painting the sky for the first time since being back in the States. A smile split my face, the muscles straining in the unfamiliar pose, and I caught a glimpse of the two of us in a window's reflection. It didn't matter that I was in a wheelchair and she was pushing me…it only mattered that the reflection showed us together.

CHAPTER 11

(JUNE – BROOKE)

The last day of school—a time of great celebration for all children...and even more so for teachers.

I plopped down in my chair, the children's exuberance on the last day of school overflowing and it was only nine o'clock in the morning. I had spent every weekend with Ethan, first traveling back and forth to Bethesda and then assisting him with getting settled in his WTU. He had made so much progress and had managed to Skype with the children on several occasions.

As soon as they discovered he had been injured, the cards, letters, and gifts flowed in. Every weekend, I took an armload to Ethan and together we distributed the baked goodies to the other recuperating soldiers.

The students were disappointed he would not be able to come see them, but he promised to visit them next school year. A secret smile slid across my face...*next school year.* We had not talked about our future, other than taking one day at a time, until he made that promise while Skyping with the class.

"What are you going to do this summer, Ms. Thompson?" Chloe asked, tugging on my arm to get my attention.

Startling, I smiled and said, "Well, I hope to take some time to enjoy the beach and maybe take a few trips."

"Are you going to see Specialist Miller?"

A commotion at the door interrupted my answer and before I turned around to see what was happening, the children began shouting. Whirling around, my gaze landed on Ethan, standing with the aid of crutches, wearing a light blue polo shirt and jeans with one leg cut off to accommodate his brace. My breath left my lungs in a rush as they locked gazes.

Tears sprang to my eyes, knowing the lengths he must have gone to to make this visit. Rushing to his side, I resisted the urge to throw my arms around him and managed to greet him properly.

His blue eyes locked on my green ones as he greeted me. Leaning in, he whispered, "Hey, babe. You're beautiful."

Beaming, I ushered him to a seat, making sure to see to his comfort. His progress had been incredible and his new physical therapist had pulled me aside one day to let me know that I had a lot to do with Ethan's renewed enthusiasm.

"How did you get here?"

"Old fashioned way...I took a cab. That'll have to do until I can drive again."

I gathered the children around his chair, but he interrupted them just as they were beginning to introduce themselves.

"No, no, let me," he insisted. Looking carefully at the expectant faces gazing up at him, he pointed to each one, calling out their correct name. The students cheered as he named the last one and I battled back the tears of joy.

The questions began to fly and soon Ethan was telling

them everything they wanted to know. He shied away from exactly what happened in the explosion, simply letting them know that sometimes soldiers got hurt during war. I watched as they accepted his answers and breathed a sigh of relief that they had not upset him.

The hour flew by and it was time for the students to go to lunch. Lining them up at the door, they each said goodbye to Ethan as they walked out with their lunch-boxes, heading to the cafeteria.

Nicole, the last to leave, looked up into Ethan's smiling face as she said goodbye. Then to my surprise, she turned back and asked, "Are you going to marry Ms. Thompson?"

"Nicole!" I gasped, my face burning.

Chuckling, Ethan leaned forward as much as he was able, and asked, "Do you think I should?"

"Oh, yes!" the little girl enthused. "She smiles whenever we talked about you and was so sad when you stopped writing."

Grinning, he stood up straight and winked at Nicole as she hurried to catch up with her class.

Turning back to me now that we were the only two left in the room, he set one crutch against the doorframe as he balanced on the other one. Lifting his free hand, he ordered gently, "Come here, babe."

Stepping closer, I slid my hand to his chest, staring up into his face as he took my lips. Aware of our surroundings, he kept the kiss light, but licked my lips as he pulled back.

"I'm almost ready to transition out of WTU," he said, "and should be ready to interview with the naval base nearby for a civilian job."

Beaming ear to ear, I asked, "So, you're going to need a place to stay."

Nodding, his smile slipped as he said, "Yeah, but I'm

going to need to find one that's handicapped accessible...or has an elevator."

"You've never been to my apartment," I said, my eyes twinkling.

Tilting his head to the side, he said, "Your apartment?"

"Well, you know I never got a roommate. But what I didn't tell you is that it's a first-floor apartment that was built handicapped accessible. The second bedroom has a large, walk-in shower stall with bars on the wall."

Pulling me closer until I was once more plastered against his front, he asked, "Any particular reason you're telling me this?"

Lifting my shoulders in a little shrug, I grinned. "I thought maybe you'd like to check it out...see if you wanted to move in with me."

With a whoop, he kissed me once more leaving me glad we were alone in the room.

* * *

(Ethan)

After dismissing the cab, I stayed in the school until the end of the day, enjoying both the students and seeing Brooke work her magic in the classroom. After the children had left for the year and she secured her room for the summer, we climbed into her car. She pushed the passenger seat as far back as she could and, since my knee would now bend, I fit nicely.

As she pulled into the parking space of her apartment, she admitted butterflies were battling in her stomach.

Sucking in a deep breath, she startled when I placed my hand over hers.

"Listen, babe," I said. "You do not have to feel obligated to have me here, just because—"

"No, no, Ethan, that's not it," she interrupted, biting her lip. "I don't want you to feel smothered...or obligated either."

"I know it seems like we're new, but I fell for you a long time ago," I said, squeezing her hand as I held her gaze.

Nodding slowly, she looked into my eyes and I felt myself drowning in her gaze. "Me too," she whispered.

"All right, then let's go look at *our* place."

* * *

Lying on my back in the middle of Brooke's bed, my eyes perused the beautiful woman presenting herself to me. We'd barely made it into her apartment, before kissing once more. This time, with no children as an audience, there had been no reason to stop.

Balancing on crutches, I'd held her face in my hands as I devoured her lips. Soft and sexy, sweet and strong, I was intoxicated with the taste of her. Finally pulling away slightly, I peered down into her lust-filled eyes.

"Do you—"

"Yeah," she answered before I finished. Licking her kiss-swollen lips, she blushed. "That is if you want—"

"Hell, yeah," I whispered, my breath washing over her face.

Smiling, she led me into her bedroom then turned, her brow furrowed. "Um...how can we—"

"If you can handle being on top, I think we can manage." I hesitated, wanting her more than anything, but not wanting our first time to be awkward.

Brooke, seeming to understand my reticence, turned to face me, looking up into my eyes. Smiling, she said, "We got this. All that matters right now is you and me...together."

Stepping back, she pulled her shirt over her head and dropped it onto the floor. I stared at her breasts, confined in their pink lacy bra and my cock swelled even more. She slipped her pants off, snagging her panties along the way. With a quick twist of her hands, her bra fell away as well, leaving her completely naked for my perusal.

"Oh, sweetheart, you are so gorgeous," I breathed, my voice reverent in awe. Glancing down at my crutches and heavy leg brace, I moaned, "This is so messed up."

She moved directly to where her nipples touched my chest and smiled as she placed her hands on my shoulders. "No, it's not. Whatever we do will be perfect, because it's us." She unbuttoned my polo and, with a little effort, drew it over my head. My chest and abs were well defined and she dragged her fingers over the ridges, drawing a hiss from my lips.

Emboldened, she unbuttoned my jeans and worked them carefully down my leg and over the brace. Pulling my boxers down as well, she freed my engorged cock, a drop of pre-cum already leaking. Maneuvering me to sit on the edge of the bed, she worked my jeans and boxers off my feet and watched as I scooted back onto the bed.

"Condom," I managed to say, and watched as she bent to grab one from my pant's pocket. Taking it from her, I rolled it on quickly, my hands shaking with anticipation and desire.

I caught a flash of uncertainty cross her face and rushed, "Brooke, we don't have to do anything you don't want to."

Her face softened as she shook her head. "No, no, it's not that. I just don't want to hurt you."

"You won't...I promise. But let me take care of you first."

Swinging her leg over my hips, she settled at the tip of my cock. "I'm ready," she said and, as I brought my hand to her folds, I felt the moisture and grinned.

Together we guided her hips down until she was impaled on my erection, the sense of fullness for her and tightness for me causing both of us to groan at the same time. It took a few tries for Brooke to get over her fear of hurting my leg and develop the rocking motion that brought us the friction we craved.

I could not take my eyes off her. Long blonde hair hung in a sheet, providing a private curtain. Her face, even more beautiful in pleasure, enraptured me. My hands held her breasts as I tweaked her nipples, drawing moans from her lips.

While I first concentrated on keeping my leg still, my mind soon slid into the place where all I felt was my aching cock moving in her slick channel. Her inner muscles gripped me tightly and I felt the pressure building in my lower back, knowing I was close.

* * *

(Brooke)

I felt the tightness in my core as sparks began tingling outward in all directions. With my hands on Ethan's shoulders, my eyes closed in ecstasy, I rocked back and forth, my breasts bouncing in rhythm with my movements.

Reaching his hand down, he pressed his thumb on my

clit, eliciting the reaction we both desired. My fingers dug into his shoulder muscles as I cried out my release.

Waves of tremors pulsated through my orgasm as my sex tightened around his cock, and I cried out his name. My eyes flew open, my green eyes piercing his blue ones as he pumped upwards a few more times until roaring out his own release.

Laying on his chest, heartbeat to heartbeat, I slowly regained my wits and attempted to move off his body.

His arms tightened, but I protested, "I don't want to hurt you."

"Baby, the only thing you could do to hurt me now is to leave."

Relaxing back on his chest, my head tucked next to his, I cupped his strong jaw in my hand. "Never," I promised.

"I love you, Brooke," he whispered, his voice still strained with the exertion, but his smile warming my heart.

CHAPTER 12

(DECEMBER - ETHAN)

I watched her, with tears in my eyes, as she walked down the aisle on the arm of her dad. My breath caught in my throat and I had to remind myself to breathe. As she placed her hand in mine, I squeezed her fingers as we turned to the minister. Twenty minutes later, the ceremony came to a close.

"I now pronounce you husband and wife. You may kiss your bride."

At those words, I grinned as I dipped Brooke backward and kissed her, long and hard. The cheering from the wedding guests finally registered and had me pull her back up, kissing her nose for good measure.

Linking fingers, we walked back down the aisle of friends, family, and a large group of ten-year-olds.

Later, at the reception, I walked over to Jon, clapping him on the back and said, "Glad you could make it, man."

"Timing was perfect. My tour was up a month ago and I figured I'd come this way for your wedding and maybe see about a job at the naval base also."

"Absolutely! When I get back from my honeymoon, I'll talk to my supervisor."

"I can't believe how good your leg is," Jon commented. "When I saw you on the ground, I wasn't sure you were even alive." He dropped his chin, shaking his head. "Fuckin' hell, man, you scared the shit outta me!"

"Hell, nine months ago, I never thought I would walk without a limp either!" I stared into my friend's eyes and added, "You know, I've never thanked you for getting in touch with Brooke. I owe you, man."

Glancing over at my bride, Jon just grinned. "Well, if she's got any hot, single friends, maybe you can hook me up. Especially if one of them bakes cookies!"

As Brooke danced with her father, her mother moved to my side. Lifting her gaze to me, she smiled as we slid our arms around each other, watching the dance in the middle of the floor. "I remember when Brooke first told me she was falling for a soldier she had not even met."

"Mrs. Thompson, I'm sure you weren't happy about that," I stated honestly, wondering what my response as a father would have been, then grimacing when I realized I would have probably said *over my dead body!*

Chuckling, she shook her head and replied, "Brooke was always so careful...so cautious. And while I was surprised, I knew she would make the right choice." Holding my gaze for a moment, she said, "And I think she has. Welcome to the family, Ethan."

The two of us hugged just as Brooke and her father finished their dance. Making my way back over to my beautiful wife, I slid my arm around her waist, and nuzzled her neck. "You ready?" I asked, my breath warm against her ear.

(Brooke and Ethan)

Nodding, Brooke grinned as she and Ethan walked toward the tables holding the excited former-students. She couldn't believe it, but all twenty-four of the children's parents brought them to the wedding. Walking around giving and receiving heartfelt hugs, she and Ethan finally stood in front of her former class, proposing a toast. The children lifted their glasses of apple juice and grinned at the couple.

"Ms. Thompson, who is now Mrs. Miller, and I are so grateful to each one of you. Not only were you a great class last year, but you became very necessary to me when I was in the Army...and then when I was hurt. So, we want to toast you for helping to bring us together." As Brooke and Ethan held their flutes filled with apple juice as well, he called out, "Here's to a class of love!"

With shouts and cheers ringing in his ear, he kissed his bride once more.

SIGN OF LOVE

Bonus Story
Letters From Home Series

By
Maryann Jordan

Sign of Love (Letters From Home Series)
Copyright 2017 Maryann Jordan

CHAPTER 1

(NOVEMBER – BECKY)

Marble is hard. And icy marble is cold. Hard. Cold. Miserable. Just like me.

The clouds covered most of the sun as the brisk wind blew my long, blonde hair about my face. I sat stiffly on the white, marble bench on top of the hill as I snuggled deeper into my coat, my red scarf pulled up over my nose. Matching red, knit gloves attempted to warm my hands but their iciness came from within. The red was the only flash of color in the scenery. My gaze moved across the grassy knoll of the cemetery, the various shapes and sizes of tombstones dotting the landscape, as familiar to me as my own home. Finally, my gaze dropped to the stone directly in front of me.

Sergeant Robert Timothy Belton
Beloved Son...Beloved Soldier

I twisted the diamond ring on my left hand around as I viewed the words on the grey marble and thought of the title that was missing. *Beloved Fiancé.* Heaving a sigh, I wiped a familiar tear from my cheek, thinking of what should have been happening on this very day. Our wedding.

"It would have been right about now, Robbie," I said, my voice carrying in the wind. "We would be standing in the church, saying our vows, and getting ready to party with our friends."

Closing my eyes, I envisioned the reception hall of my small church, ivory bunting draped from the center of the room, billowing out to wind around the pillar support beams. The three-tiered cake would be setting on a round table in the corner, decorated with pink flowers of fondant and buttercream frosting. Guests would move around the room, partaking in the buffet tables laden with the delights the women of the church would have provided. It was going to be a simple affair...but exactly what we had planned. My dress had been bought and still hung in its garment bag, never to see the light of day. *If only...*

If only you had not gone back for one last tour...If only you had not volunteered one more time...if only you had come back to me, alive and whole, ready for our wedding...instead of here.

The sound of voices lifted in singing Amazing Grace reached my ears and I turned to look down the hill behind me. From my perch, I was able to see the familiar funeral tent over a flag draped casket, surrounded by flowers. Glad that the service was not close to where I sat, I twisted back to stare straight ahead. I had my own grief to deal with and no desire to observe someone else's.

I came here often in the past six months...at first I came every day and then gradually my visits slowed to once a week. The cemetery officials knew me well and waved as I drove my little car out here to sit with Robbie. *Well, Robbie's gravesite.* My mother worried about me coming so often, sitting alone in all types of weather, just to talk to him. But Robbie would understand. He would know exactly what I was doing. And why. He'd always understood me.

There had never been a time when he hadn't been in my life. Our families lived next door to each other and my baby pictures included us laying in the same crib when our moms visited every day. And so began the life of Robbie and me, well documented over the years in photographs. Pictures of us playing in our yards, swinging on an old tire swing, dressing up for trick or treating, playing ball, and eventually Robbie in his high school football uniform and me in my cheerleading outfit. Our bedrooms faced each other and late at night we would open our windows and call out. Even when we had cellphones, we still opened our windows just so we could have that connection.

We were perfect together...everyone said so. And destined to be married...everyone expected it.

And now? I lifted my head toward the heavens as the darker clouds rolled in, sighing once again knowing I had no answer to that question. When you've lost the one thing you've had your whole life, what do you do?

The jarring sound an honor guard team firing three volleys from rifles, jolted me from my musings. The shock resounded throughout my body causing my heart to pound. Tears sprang to my eyes, the memory of the honor salute given during Robbie's funeral. I hated the sound. I know what it represented. I know the time-honored tradition was supposed to be special. But to me, the jolt of the rifle fire solidified the horror of my loss.

Unable to keep from looking over my shoulder again, I watched as the flag was folded and presented to a woman seated near the casket. Too far to determine if it was a wife or a mother, my heart ached for their grief nonetheless. I remember Robbie's flag being given to his mother as she sat next to me at his funeral. My fingers had itched to hold it too, but it wasn't for me.

As the crowd below dispersed, I watched the cars snake back through the meandering road of the cemetery and reveled in the quiet once they were gone. I knew the cemetery would soon begin the noisy process of interring the casket and taking down the tent and chairs…I'd spent enough time on this bench to have the whole process memorized having witnessed it numerous times. Reaching into my bag, I pulled out my earbuds and turned on the music. The sad, romantic, instrumental music that always left me in tears. Today I added something special to my playlist…the song we planned to dance to at our wedding reception. I lay my head against the tombstone and closed my eyes.

Sliding off the cold marble, I knelt on the grass next to Robbie's tombstone and allowed my fingers to glide over the letters in his name. **Belton**. That was going to be my last name. I used to write Rebecca Anne Belton in the margins of my notebooks in high school. That habit continued at the college I attended. Leaning my head down so that my forehead rested against the smooth headstone, I closed my eyes as the sad music floated through me, memories mixed with wishes of what would have been.

* * *

(Caleb)

The sound of rifle fire zinged through me, filling me with a sense of pride. Standing at attention, I faced the flag draped coffin, swallowing deeply. The chilly air filled my lungs as I watched the flag folded and presented to Tim's mom. Her grief-ravaged face nodded slightly toward the honor guard as she clutched the flag to her chest, tears dropping from her chin onto the cloth.

As the funeral ended and the mourners moved back to their cars, Tim's father walked over, his hand extended toward me. As he took my hand, his mother moved in and wrapped one arm around her husband's waist while the other still clung to the flag. As the three of us hugged, I closed my eyes, stinging with unshed tears, as I tried to offer strength to his parents. I was feeling many things at that moment, but strength wasn't one of them.

His mother leaned back, her tear-stained face turned up toward me. "Oh, Caleb, we're so glad you were able to accompany Tim back. He spoke of you in his letters and we know you were such a good friend to him."

"There's no where else I'd rather be, ma'am. I'm honored to be here, but just so sorry for the reason."

"We'll see you at the wake, son?" Mr. Scarsdale asked.

I actually hated the idea of sitting in a closed space, surrounded by Tim's grieving relatives and was glad for the excuse. "I'll be flying back soon, sir, so I'll say my good-byes now."

I watched the two move slowly to their car, after we hugged goodbye and they accepted my condolences once more. Leaning on each other for support, they finally drove away, leaving me as the sole mourner. Only then did I allow myself to turn back to the casket. Placing my hand on the polished wood, I said goodbye...to my squad member, my bunkmate, my friend. The cemetery workers stepped back, willing to let me have this time. I'd seen men die—had friends injured—but Tim was my closest friend and I couldn't imagine going back to the war without him by my side. Sucking in a deep breath of cold air, I blew it out, the frost leaving a trail from my lips.

With a final nod, I turned and walked toward my rental car noticing there was one other car parked farther down the road. Standing for a moment, I allowed the cool breeze to flow over me as I looked around. The cemetery was old but well maintained. Trees dotted the area and marble benches were placed randomly, allowing mourners to sit while visiting.

As my gaze drifted up toward a small hill, I noticed a lone figure leaning, unmoving, near a headstone. I continued to watch to make sure the person was all right, but they never moved. *Are they ill?* Concerned, I walked up the hill, careful to stay on the path between gravesites. Approaching the still woman, I wondered if she was conscious. Reaching over, I touched her shoulder.

Her screech pierced the quiet as she flipped around, landing on her ass quicker than I've ever seen a human move. Wide-eyed, she stared up at me as she crab-scrambled backward.

Throwing my hands up, I stepped back. "I'm sorry, I'm sorry," I babbled, warring between the desire to assist her up and declaring my innocence. We stared at each other for a moment, uncertainty filling the air between us.

She was much younger than I first imagined. Her dark blonde hair blowing in the breeze stood out in stark contrast to the black coat she was wearing. Brown eyes stared back at me and I observed the dried tear trail on her pale cheek. Slim wires came from her ears and I noticed earbuds. *That's why she didn't hear me.* Her mouth opened and I braced for another scream.

"What…who…?" she stammered, lifting one hand to jerk the earbuds out.

"Ma'am, I'm so sorry," I rushed, kneeling close by so she

did not have to look up so far at me while I kept a respectable distance. "I saw you up here and was afraid you were ill. I apologize for scaring you."

Her pink tongue darted out, licking her lips before sucking them in, her chest rising and falling rapidly. I stuck my hand out warily and she eyed it suspiciously.

"Please, ma'am, let me assist you up and then I promise to leave you to your...uh...well, I'll leave. I just want to make sure you're all right."

She hesitated for a moment before reaching her hand out and placing it in mine. Her delicate touch sent shivers through my arm. *It must be her cold fingers* I surmised, but as I clamped my hand around hers and gently pulled her upward as I stood, it was warmth, not cold, that moved up my arm into my chest. Now standing, I could see she was petite, the top of her head below my chin as her head tilted back, her eyes still on mine.

"I'm Caleb Winters, ma'am. Sergeant Caleb Winters."

She licked her lips again in what I was sure was a nervous gesture but I suddenly focused on her pink lips. No longer concerned that she was ill, I now observed how beautiful she was. A slight pull on my hand and I realized I still had her fingers clasped in mine. Dropping them suddenly, I missed the warmth from her touch.

Nodding slowly, her gaze moved over my uniform, as she tucked a fly-about strand of hair behind her ear. Speaking softly, she replied, "Thank you for checking on me, Sergeant Winters. That was kind of you."

My eyes now dropped to the headstone she had been leaning against. Sergeant Robert Timothy Belton. *Is that her brother? A relative? Husband?* The date indicated he had died six months earlier and only mentioned son and soldier.

She noted the line of my gaze and her chin lifted

slightly as she swallowed deeply, but offered no explanation.

"Well, if you're sure you're all right…" my voice trailed off, the desire to not leave her alone overwhelming.

Ducking her head, her lips curved ever so slightly. "Yes, thank you." Sighing, she leaned down to pick up her bag, throwing it over her shoulder. "I should be leaving as well."

Turning, I instinctively offered her my arm, watching the hesitation in her eyes for only a second before she slid her hand through the crook at my elbow. Making sure to walk carefully on the slick grass, I escorted her down to the only other car in the vicinity.

Stopping at the driver's door, I reluctantly let go of her arm, wanting to stay and talk. Whoever she was grieving for, I felt a strong connection to the emotion. And the truth was, her beauty called to me as well.

Her head turned back toward Tim's gravesite where the cemetery workers were busy with their post funeral jobs.

"I always hate this part," she said, her voice so low I had to strain to hear her words. "I come here often and have the chance to see what happens after the family leaves." She turned her face back to me, adding, "It's all very respect-ful…it's just…I don't know…lonely." Looking at her feet for a moment, she signed deeply.

Lifting her gaze once more, she said, "I'm sorry for your loss. I know everyone says that…but I really am. So very sorry for your loss."

I felt the sting of unshed tears at her words and forced my gaze to tear away from Tim's busy gravesite and focus back on her. She turned to open her car door and I suddenly knew I needed to stay in her presence for a little longer.

"I have to catch a flight in a couple of hours, but would you have a cup of coffee with me first?" I blurted, immediately contrite at the ridiculousness of the request. *Why would she want to have coffee...she's just been grieving herself and has no clue who I am!*

I started to retract the offer when she pierced me with her thoughtful gaze and slowly nodded. "Yeah...that would be nice."

My breath left my body in a whoosh—it felt like a reprieve to a condemned man. Before I could speak again, she said, "There's a small coffee shop a few blocks from here. You could follow me."

Eagerly agreeing, I assisted her into her car and jogged over to mine. With one last look back at Tim's grave, I felt my heart squeeze in grief before turning back to follow the woman out of the cemetery. Then I realized...I didn't even know her name.

CHAPTER 2

(BECKY)

Am I crazy? I've just agreed to meet a complete stranger for coffee! When I landed on my ass next to Robbie's headstone, startled and gazing up at the soldier standing over me, I was sure he could hear my heart pounding. At first I thought it was because I was frightened. Then I assumed it was because of the uniform and the reminder of Robbie. But as I continued to stare up at his face, his brows drawn down in concern, a warmth spread through me. His brown hair was cut military-short. He was tall...and broad. A square jaw sported full lips, slightly turned down in a frown.

And now, as I drove out of the cemetery toward town, glancing in the rearview mirror to see him following me, I had to admit that I was curious. Curious about the man in the uniform and who he just buried today. I was no expert on grief but for the last six months I had become well acquainted with the emotion that kicked my ass every day.

Before I had time to process further, I parked outside a small coffee shop in a shopping center hesitating as I second-guessed my decision. *This is a public place so I should be safe here.* Hearing another car, I noticed he parked next to me. We alighted from our vehicles at the same time and silently walked toward the shop.

I felt his hand resting gently on the small of my back. It's a strange gesture…one that Robbie never did, but I had to admit I liked. It didn't feel possessive…nor did it feel patronizing. It sent warmth through me and made me feel less alone. It just seemed…comforting. *Maybe it's been too long since I've felt anything comforting.*

Stepping inside the welcoming interior of the shop, the scent of roasting coffee beans and flavored syrups immediately greeted us as we walked to the counter and ordered our drinks. His hand settled at my back once again as we walked to a small table in the corner. Unbuttoning my coat, I felt him reach for the material and slide it down my arms.

Turning, I offered a small smile as I faced him. "Sergeant Winters, I haven't even introduced myself." Seeing him grin, I stuck my hand out and said, "I'm Rebecca Adams, but everyone calls me Becky."

He clasped my hand in his much larger one again, his smile showing white teeth and dimples. "It's nice to meet you, Becky," he said, still smiling. "And please call me Caleb." I jolted when the server walked over with our coffees a minute later and realized we had been standing in statue-like stillness, our hands still joined.

I felt the heat of blush rise over my face as I pulled my hand back and slid into my chair, wrapping my hands around the steaming cup. Caleb sat across from me, looking down at his coffee before lifting his gaze back to me. "I really appreciate you coming with me." Glancing back down, he continued, "Today was harder than I thought it would be."

Now that we were closer, I stared at the man sitting

across from me. The white shirt stood out in crisp relief against the blue jacket, ribbons and badges adorning the front. I recognized the sergeant stripes, remembering when Robbie had earned his. For a second, staring at his chest, I could have forgotten who was at my table, but then lifted my gaze and the difference was striking. Robbie had light blond hair while Caleb's was dark brown. And the blue eyes of my fiancé were not looking back at me. Instead, hazel eyes pierced me, suffering clearly in their depths.

I cleared my throat while clearing my thoughts at the same time. "Do you mind telling me who's funeral you were attending?" I asked, curiosity overcoming shyness.

A flash of pain flew through his eyes before he replied, "It was one of my squad mates. We'd known each other since boot camp and he was killed last week."

"Afghanistan?"

Caleb nodded before turning the question around to me. "And you? Who were you visiting?"

I hesitated, always hating to say it out loud, as though that made it more real, more definite...or maybe I should say more final. But Caleb had been so forthcoming, it would be cowardly of me not to reply. "Robbie was my fiancé. And..." I hesitated, "today was to be our wedding day."

Caleb's eyes widened as he gasped. "Oh, Becky, I'm so sorry. Truly sorry." He reached out and placed his hand over mine, squeezing my fingers. "I would have never interrupted your time at the cemetery if I had known—"

"Oh, no, I'm glad you did," I assured him and realized that I was truly glad. My tears from earlier were spent and the ache in my heart, while always there, ached just a little less. "I had my cry at the cemetery and now I think it's good to have a diversion on this day," I explained.

Nodding, he said, "Good." Then silent for a moment, he added, "I think maybe we both needed a diversion today."

Relaxing back in my chair, I agreed while sipping my coffee. "When Robbie first died, I wanted to talk about him all the time. I don't know if you feel the same, but if so, please tell me about your friend...if you want to."

"He was a good man," Caleb said, leaning back, his gaze on his cup but I knew his mind was somewhere in the past. "That sounds trite, like I can't come up with another description and am just looking for an out. But he honestly was a really good man. We met in boot camp and went into the same MOS...uh...Military Occupational Specialties... uh, that means our job—"

"I know," I smiled softly. "Robbie was in the Army."

"Oh, yeah...sorry," Caleb mumbled. Running his hand over his face, he said, "Listen, you don't want to hear about this."

I reached out and placed my hand over his. "Yes, really I do. I need a diversion, remember?"

Sighing in understanding, his eyes met mine and I felt strange, as though a physical connection passed between us beyond just our hands. Swallowing quickly, I said, "Please...go on."

With a slight squeeze of his fingers on mine, he continued. "We were both Military Police. It was our second tour in Afghanistan. He was..." looking back up at me, he said, "He was a good soldier. And I know that sounds just as simple as saying he was a good man. Why is that?"

"Because we want them to be here with us so badly that everything we say feels disingenuous."

His eyes widened as he nodded vigorously, agreeing, "Yes! You're right. I want to talk about him but then feel angry that I'm talking about him in past tense!"

My shoulders slumped and I sat quietly...there was nothing to say. His words had been felt by me for months.

"Tim was always one of those people who was up for a fun time and hated to see anyone down. He kept my spirits up more than anyone. He was the first to volunteer for a mission and would have your back if you were lucky to be working with him."

I sipped my coffee, letting Caleb talk about his friend, knowing he needed this time.

After a while, his words slowed down as his gaze stayed on his hands lying on the table. Finally looking up, he said, "I want to thank you again for coming out with me," and I noticed his eyes no longer held the specter of pain. "I dreaded this afternoon and you've made it much more bearable."

"I haven't spoken this much to anyone in a long time," I confessed, my heart feeling strangely lighter, "so I thank you as well. It's been nice to talk about Robbie and to hear about Tim. I'd say we both needed this."

Looking at his watch, he sighed heavily. "I really hate to leave, but I do have to get the rental car back to the airport in time to make my flight."

He stood and once more, reached his hand out for me. I stared for only a second as a flash of Robbie in his uniform flew through my mind again. Blinking, I gazed up at Caleb's face as I took his hand, allowing him to assist me from my chair. Instead of feeling guilty, I was awash in warmth and an unfamiliar feeling of peace. In helping Caleb, I felt more alive than I had in months. Six months to be exact.

* * *

(Caleb)

121

I had no idea what was happening, but I was desperate to not lose the connection with Becky as I stood behind her, slipping her coat onto her shoulders. The dark coat once again covered the pale green sweater and dark, wool pants. I watched as she lifted her blonde tresses from under her coat collar and my fingers itched to slide through the silken strands. She turned around, smiling up at me with her sweet pink lips tempting my desire to kiss her. *What the hell am I thinking? This was supposed to be her wedding day...the last thing she'd want is me taking advantage of her.*

Forcing my thoughts away from her lips, I placed my hand on her back as I escorted her outside to her car. *I don't want this to end!* I had only met her, but the desire to spend more time with her was overwhelming. I observed her carefully as she stood next to her car door, trying to read her thoughts. *Anything...give me anything, Becky...*

She hesitated, not immediately opening the door. Opening her mouth and closing it a couple of times, I was certain she wanted to say something.

Deciding to take a chance, I asked, "Would it be possible to get your email address?" My heart beat a cadence in my chest as I observed the play of emotions cross her face. Just as I was ready to let her off the hook, her smile grew wider.

"Yeah," she answered, her face more beautiful with a soft smile playing about her lips. "I was just thinking that I'd like to be able to talk to you more also."

My relief was visible as my breath rushed out. "Great!" I pulled out my phone and entered her email as she rattled it off for me. As she finished, I noted she had pulled her phone out of her purse and was staring expectantly at me as well. "Oh, yeah," I grinned and spelled it out for her.

She met my smile and I was struck once more with her

beauty. In the cemetery, she seemed so delicate...almost fragile. Now with the warm drink giving her pale cheeks some color and a light shining in her eyes, she appeared stronger. I knew I would email and hoped she would reply.

"Well," I began, sticking my hand out, "I guess this is goodbye." As the words left my mouth, my heart dropped.

She reached out, her small hand in mine, and nodded. "I guess it is." Then, in a stunning move, she stood on her tiptoes, kissing my cheek, and whispered, "Be safe," before turning and opening her car door. Sliding into the driver's seat, she looked up and said, "I'll write. I promise." With that she blinked quickly before one lone tear slid down her cheek as she pulled out of the parking lot.

I stood, alone and lonely, on the sidewalk, my mind running over the day's surprising turn of events. From the angst of Tim's funeral, to the concern of the beautiful, grieving woman, to the hour we spent chatting. And now she's gone and I have to head back to the other side of the world. Looking back down at my phone, seeing her email, I grinned, knowing I had a way to keep in contact with her.

* * *

Thirty-six hours later, having traveled half-way around the world, reported in, and then crashed when I first got back to base, I headed to the Morale, Welfare, and Recreation tent to send an email to Becky. I tried to convince myself that meeting her had simply made a shitty day better...but I knew it was more than that. She had touched me deep inside, with both her understanding of my grief and the sadness in her eyes that I wanted to erase.

Sitting down at the computer station, I pulled up my email. Quickly deleting the spam, I caught sight of her email address…in my inbox. Gasping a sharp breath, my finger jumped to click the mouse.

Dear Caleb,

I guess you're surprised that I emailed first, but I just had to tell you how much it meant to me to meet you today. I had dreaded this day, knowing what should have been if Robbie had not died. And the tears I shed before you came over to me were needed. But if I had not met you, I would have gone home despondent—and I've spent so many hours being sad. Because my future was so planned, it's been hard to figure out where to go from here. And I've learned that grief can grind everything to a halt. So thank you for checking on me and then talking to me.

I hope that your trip back was uneventful and that you've had a chance to rest, although for soldiers I suppose you never get much time to rest. Robbie told me some about the Army but we didn't talk about it much. He was getting out before the wedding and going to work for his dad's construction company.

I know some of the feelings you are going to go through with your friend's death and if you ever want to talk about it, please do. Believe me, I've been there! I'm slowly learning that grief doesn't ever leave us, we just learn to live with it. They say time heals, but I'm not sure I believe that. I think that time just means we eventually get used to grief always being with us.

Anyway, I hope I hear from you, but if not, just know that I appreciated what you did for me today.

Becky

She wrote! Before I had a chance to send her an email, she wrote to me! Fatigue still pulled at my body but I felt lighter. The same warmth that flowed through me when we touched was now filling me once again. Unable to hide my smile, I began to type.

Dear Becky,

This will be short because I've just gotten back and still jet-lagged, plus I go back on duty tomorrow. But I wanted to tell you what a surprise it was to get your email—a really good surprise! I felt presumptuous asking you to coffee and then again for your email, but I could not stand the thought of leaving you and never talking to you again.

Meeting you gave me a chance to process some of the feelings I had about Tim...and rescue me from the reception I dreaded going to. Sometimes I think fate steps in when we least expect it.

I hope to hear from you again soon.

Caleb

CHAPTER 3

(DECEMBER – BECKY)

I was in my room but could hear the Christmas music from downstairs. Mom always began playing holiday tunes from the moment Thanksgiving was over and this year was no different. Bending back over my books, I continued studying for my last exam of the semester. Only one more semester to go and I would have my degree.

A light knock sounded on my door and at my urging, Mom stuck her head through. Her hair was still blonde and the short bob was perfect for her face. She had always been the first to smile with me, my shoulder to cry on, and my biggest champion...but for the past seven months I could tell she was worried.

"Hey, sweetheart," she greeted. "I know you're hard at work, but I made some cookies and thought you might like a break."

Smiling, I nodded. "Sure. Just let me finish this last paragraph and I'll be down." I watched relief soften the worry lines from her face as she smiled in return.

"You seem...better," she said, then ducked her head. "I'm

sorry. That probably didn't sound right. I just mean that…
oh, I don't know."

Chuckling, I replied, "I know what you mean, mom. I'm
sleeping more and crying less, so I guess that means I'm
learning to live with my grief."

Her gaze met mine as she said, "I wondered if you were
seeking help."

I hesitated, not knowing what to say. The truth is that I
had been talking to someone…Caleb. The few emails we
had shared seemed to help lift my burden as he encouraged
me to talk about Robbie and I learned more about Tim.
Not wanting to share that newfound friendship yet, I just
smiled as I replied, "I think staying busy has done a lot to
keep me sane."

"Well, come down when you can," she said, before
closing me door once again.

Looking around the room for a moment, I shook my
head. Twenty-three years old and living back in my old
room. This had never been in my plans. I had moved from
the dorms after two years in college and had a small apartment for the next couple of years. Robbie and I decorated
it together…it was to be ours when he got out of the Army.
Every leave he got, we would spend more time making it
our place.

And when he was killed…I couldn't stay there. As the
walls had closed in on me, my parents came to my rescue
and brought me back to their house. They took care of
packing up and moving the furniture into storage, and so
for seven months I had lived back in my old bedroom. The
twin-sized bed might have a new floral bedspread taking
the place of the hot-pink one I used to have, but it was still
the bed of my childhood. The walls were cream, repainted
from my pink and purple phase and now sported a couple

of paintings instead of boy-bands and cheerleading pompoms, but it felt sterile.

Leaning back in my chair, I realized this space wasn't the best place for getting away from my memories, considering Robbie had spent a lot of time here with me when we were growing up. I glanced out the window seeing his parents' house and his empty, closed window facing mine. With a sigh and a mental shake, I turned back to my textbook and quickly finished the paper.

Just before closing my computer, I heard the ding of incoming email. Holding my breath, I hoped...*Yes! Caleb!* After I sent my initial email, he had quickly responded, but still jet-lagged, had kept it short. A few more emails had passed back and forth between us, each one causing a smile from me. Clicking on his name, I opened his missive.

Hey Becky,

I was really glad you told me more about Robbie and I can't imagine how difficult it has been to have to try to figure out your life now that everything you thought was going to happen has changed. I admit that Tim and I talked about getting out of the Army and getting hired on at the same police force...in fact, we even talked about getting our PI license and opening up our own business. We hadn't decided where we would move to since neither one of us felt strongly about staying in one of our hometowns. That part was open, but the rest of our plans were more solid. And now, I have to think about my professional future without him as well as miss him as a friend.

I've been thinking about what you said about grief being a journey that we have to travel. Those words resonated with me and made a lot of sense. I know Tim

would want me to keep planning for my future, but I have to figure out what that is now.

You asked about being a military policeman. It's a lot different from being a civilian policeman. We do a lot of the jobs they do, but then we're the ones who patrol the outer areas of the camp, drive through hostile areas to secure them, and are responsible for transporting the people who need escorting from one place to another on land. There's lots more but this just gives you a little idea.

I know you said you didn't ask Robbie about his job in the military but don't feel guilty about that. As much as I'm sure he loved you, he wouldn't have wanted you to worry. Instead, I'm sure he would have been happy to know that you were back home, planning your wedding.

Since I don't know your age, I wondered if you knew Tim at all growing up. I didn't get to see much of the town the day of his funeral, so I don't know how big it was. I thought later that you might have been acquainted. His parents seemed real nice – he always spoke highly of his family. That was another thing we had in common.

You must be almost through with your semester and I hope you enjoy your holidays. They try to make things special over here, but we're still very aware that we are far from home. I hope you have a wonderful Christmas...you deserve to find some happiness.

Caleb

Unable to keep the smile from my face, I closed my laptop and headed downstairs, ready to taste mom's cookies. As I sat at the table, the snickerdoodle's chewy goodness filling my mouth, Caleb's words came back to me. *Far from home... try to make things special.* He deserves something special. As I grabbed another cookie on my way back to my computer, my heart was lighter with the beginnings of a plan.

* * *

(Caleb)

The squad's early morning meeting came to a close as they finished discussing the day's mission. I moved to the M1117 Guardian Armored Security Vehicle, climbing into the passenger side. Richard hauled into the driver's seat as another team member crawled into the back, along with our passenger, a high ranking official needing to get to a meeting across Kabul. Three other ASVs, each with a passenger, were in the convoy.

As we drove through the base gates, my attention was focused on the threats in the city. In a world where driving rules did not exist for most drivers, pedestrians walked in the streets among the vehicles and children played in the roads. The constant threat of IEDs or attack, kept all of us on high alert. The drive through the crowded, dusty streets took longer than we hoped as traffic snarled at several junctions.

It was sometimes difficult to keep my eyes on all the movement around, as the mass of humanity would press into the streets. I'd never been to New York City, but I used to be amazed at pictures of crowds of people rushing into the intersections when the traffic lights would change. My smaller hometown didn't have many pedestrians and certainly not anything to resemble a mass. But here, the people did not even wait for vehicles to pass before rushing everywhere.

The buildings on either side of the road had the same tan exterior that almost everything in this country had. Sometimes I wondered if they were made of brick, stone, or mud, although I think many of them had all three building materials in them. Some more dilapidated than others, appeared to be standing by a miracle alone. Others appeared more substantial, but danger could come from either of them.

Outside many of the shops, men would sit at small, makeshift tables drinking or smoking, in groups of friends. My non-trusting instincts would eye them warily as we passed, checking for sudden movements. Heaving a sigh, I realized I was tired of constantly having to be suspicious of people and their motives.

Our armored vehicles finally crossed through security at the gates of a smaller base where we delivered the officials. Without needing to wait, we immediately left, taking on a patrol mission as we made our way back through the streets. Groups of children ran along the huge vehicles. Stopping occasionally to toss some candy to them, we moved on. Changing directions, we drove up and down several different roads, finally making it to base. Leaning back in my seat in relief, I was pleased for a mission completed without a hitch or an incident.

At the end of the shift I jogged between the tan tents all erected in straight lines, stopping by the mail tent. The last email from Becky hinted that she was sending something once I gave her my mailing address. And, since my squad member told me I had a package, I had a hard time waiting for the end of the day.

Entering the large tent with sand bags stacked outside the door, I saw the long, wooden counter near the back with several people in line. Working my way forward I gave my identification to the Private working behind the counter. Taking the box from her, I walked back to my tent, grinning at the thought of Becky taking the time to mail something to me. Entering, I was glad to see the space empty as I walked to my bed. Quickly opening the box, I eagerly dug inside, discovering well-packed, homemade cookies. Opening a bag, the scent of cinnamon sugar hit me as I pulled out an oversized snickerdoodle. Taking a bite, I groaned in pleasure. Pure heaven. Looking back in the box, I pulled out several bags of cookies, some toiletries, candy, gum, and at the bottom...*Jackpot*...a letter.

Setting the box to the side, I ripped open the envelope.

Dear Caleb,

I hope the cookies get to you, still fresh and not too broken. I thought that you might enjoy something special from home.

The holidays will be hard this year. We live next door to Robbie's parents and for as long as I can remember, our two families have spent Christmas Eve together. This year, I was dreading the day, but they have decided to take a trip to visit Robbie's older sister and her family in Maryland. I'm really glad...it's weird since we're all grieving, but it's different. They buried their son and that is the worst tragedy. I buried my fiancé and while I know my life will never be the same, I still have to face an uncertain future...but still a future. Maybe that doesn't make sense. Anyway, it will just be me, mom, dad for the holidays.

I never asked you where you're from. I've lived in Virginia my whole life. You asked about my semester and by the time you get this package, my exams will be over. So, only one more semester to go and I'll graduate. I'll have an education degree and will start applying for jobs. I really have no idea where I'll work. I had planned on only applying to school districts close by home since Robbie and I already had an apartment for when he returned, but now...who knows? It is weird to not be constricted in my applications and yet even that makes me feel guilty. Like maybe I should just stay here anyway.

I'll be glad to move out and into my own place again. I gave up the apartment that Robbie and I were going to share—I couldn't stand being there knowing he would never be there again. But I have to admit that the past seven months living back with my parents has been good...and difficult. They are great, but I think I'm finally ready to find my own place again. Staying in the bedroom I had as a child really isn't making moving forward any easier.

You asked it I knew Tim, but I didn't. Our city is actually mid-size and we have two high schools. If he played sports, then Robbie probably would have known him or at least heard of him. This may sound bad, but I'm glad I didn't know him. I'm not sure I could handle another death so soon after Robbie's. I confess that I worry about you. Please, please stay safe!

How much longer do you have in the Army? Have you decided what you want to do when you get out? I truly hope that you find some peace during the holidays, Caleb. Take care of yourself and be safe!

Love,

Becky

I noted her neat handwriting, smiling at her words as much as the thoughtfulness of the gifts. Leaning back against my headboard, warmth spreading throughout my body, as I continued chewing the cookie. My mom would send care packages, but this was the first time I had home-made cookies sent to me. I was struck with the irony that on what had been one of the worst days of my life, meeting

Becky had turned it into one of the best. I didn't assume that meeting me on the day she was supposed to get married would make her feel the same, but I hoped I gave her a little peace.

Please stay safe. I bolted forward as I realized what a risk she was taking in befriending me...another soldier in a warzone. Swallowing hard, I felt the weight of responsibility for my safety heavy on my shoulders. I wanted to return home for me and my parents, but now? I wanted to not cause Becky any more pain.

Leaning back again, I picked up her letter allowing my gaze to travel over the words. *Love, Becky.* I know she used the word *love* as just a common term, but I felt connected to the beautiful woman who's tears in the middle of the cemetery had touched my heart.

CHAPTER 4

(JANUARY – BECKY)

Trudging from the snow-scraped, university parking lot, I made my way to the library. I knew Robbie's parents had come back from their trip and his mom was currently ensconced in my parents' living room with my mom. Plopping down at a table in the library, I opened my laptop but sat unmoving. Sighing heavily, I felt a modicum of guilt in avoiding Robbie's mom, but uncertainty kept me away. I felt as though she wanted me to continue to grieve the way she was, but my grief was my own. Rubbing my forehead, I wished the tumultuous emotions would stop their battle in my mind.

I had written an email to Caleb, describing my mixed feelings, but after I hit send, I wondered if he thought it was cowardly of me to dread seeing Robbie's parents. Finally, awakening from my musings, I opened my email, pleased to see a reply from him.

Dear Becky,
I totally understand your desire to not immediately

see Robbie's parents. I felt guilty at not going to Tim's wake, but knew my feelings of grief were different from his relatives. And since I got to spend time with you, it was an extra special way to process my emotions over the loss.

The reality is—and I hope this doesn't come across as callous—but your feelings are going to be different from Robbie's parents. They lost a son and that will never be replaced or changed. You lost your fiancé and while he won't ever be replaced, you do have the opportunity to have another relationship with someone in your future. I know that sounds harsh and please don't think that I'm saying you'll forget him, or just move on. He will always remain in your heart. But you can love again...and I hope you do.

I guess I just want to make sure you are open to those feelings and don't close your heart off. I suppose that sounds presumptuous and I hope you're not offended.

I almost forgot to thank you for the care packages you have been sending! I share them with my squad and they are appreciative as well! My mom sends things sometimes but I get especially excited when one comes from you!

I'm from West Virginia – that's where my parents still live. My mom was upset that I flew to Virginia for Tim's funeral and didn't get to visit, but as you know I only had one day for it all. She works as a school secretary and my dad works at one of the local banks. It'll be nice to see them when I come home – mom's cooking is always worth a visit!

I get out of the Army in a couple of months and would really like to see you again. Maybe, if you agree, we can plan something.

Love,

Caleb

My mind swirled with all that he had packed into one short email. He not only understood my confused emotions surrounding Robbie's parents but gave me permission to grieve differently from them. *He's right...*as much as I loved Robbie and planned on my future with him, life intervened...but this did not mean I would never love again.

Leaning back in the hard chair of the library, I realized something profound had just moved into my heart. Looking down at my engagement ring, I knew Caleb was right...I would love again. A spear of guilt shot through me, but it was quickly followed by a sigh of reality. Robbie was gone although he would always remain in my heart.

Standing quickly, I closed my laptop and shoved it into my bag before sliding it over my shoulder. Heading back out into the frozen campus, I walked to my car. Twenty minutes later, I drove to the cemetery. The climb up the hill to Robbie's gravesite was difficult with the snow on the ground and I was glad for my sturdy boots. Arriving at the bench, I bent to brush the snow off. I stared wordlessly at the headstone, sitting on the frozen marble.

For a long time, I said nothing, the cold air matching the cold inside of me. Finally, pulling off my gloves, my gaze back to my left hand, I stared at the engagement ring. Smiling, I remembered how proud Robbie had been to slide it on my finger...and how giddy I'd been to wear it.

He had finished his first tour and I was halfway through my degree when he came home to visit. Taking me to dinner, he told me he had something important to talk to me about. I had hoped he was going to tell me that he was not re-enlisting for another tour. But as he sat across from me, the candlelight flickering between us on the table, he took my hand and before I knew what he was doing, he slid the diamond on my ring finger.

I'd cried...I'd laughed...and I'd said yes. Of course, absolutely yes.

But by the end of the evening he'd also told me that he was doing one more tour. He made it sound so perfect—he'd get out of the Army when I finished my degree and then we could continue our lives as husband and wife. I was disappointed because I wanted him near, but he supported my education so how could I not support his decision?

But that was then. And this is now. And I'm back at his gravesite.

"Robbie," I said, my eyes back on his stone, "I vowed to be your wife...and would have kept that vow. I vowed to love you forever...and I will. You will always be my first love. You will always be the man who stole my heart when we were children. But you're not here anymore and I'm left to carry on alone. It's so hard to know what to do. You've been my soulmate for my whole life."

Reaching up to unclasp my cross necklace, I laid the gold chain on my lap. Then, hesitating, my heart pounding as a tear slid down my cheek, I pulled off my engagement ring. Heaving a deep breath that left a frosty trail from my lips, I slipped the ring onto the gold chain and fastened the clasp. Now with Robbie's ring hanging around my neck, I dropped my gaze to my naked finger.

Choking back a sob, I almost grabbed the ring off the necklace to place it back on my hand...but I resisted. "I have to do this, Robbie. Please forgive me. Please know that I carry you with me in my heart forever." Swallowing deeply, I wiped my tears before tilting my face up toward the sun, allowing the brightness to filter through closed eyelids as I was assaulted by so many memories of the past.

After a few minutes, I slid from the bench to kneel at the gravestone. Placing my now ringless hand on the stone, I whispered, "I have no idea what my future holds other than you not being in it. But I promise, when I give myself to another man, it will be a good man like you...a kind man like you...a man who loves me like you did. If I'm lucky enough to find another man like that...I'll honor our love by loving him."

Standing, I kissed my fingers and touched them to the cold stone. Trudging back down the hill to my car, my gaze drifted over to Tim's gravesite. And as I climbed into my car, the thought crossed my mind...*have I already met that man?*

CHAPTER 5

(CALEB)

Two months to go…that's it. Only two more months to go. In Afghanistan. In the Army. In the freezing cold and blistering heat. In the danger with those who'd like nothing more than to kill anyone wearing our uniform.

And then…I wanted to meet up with Becky again.

Our weekly emails had increased to several times a week and my heart was undoubtedly involved. Smart, beautiful, brave, and resilient. She was the whole package. *Can this be real? Can someone fall in love with only one meeting and multiple emails?*

Tim and I had made plans for when we got out, but now I needed to figure out what to do on my own. We'd talked about either joining a police force or working toward our private investigator license. I had always planned moving back to West Virginia but now—

"Winters!" came the shout from another MP in my squad, interrupting my thoughts. "We're up."

Heading to the command post, I joined the others as we suited up in our full uniforms. Body armor. Headgear. Weapons checked and secured.

Heading out for guard gate duty, we spread out to our different responsibilities. Some of us were assigned to check the IDs of the incoming vehicles. Some walked around the vehicles with long-handled mirrors to check for bombs. And a few of us walked the perimeter of the gate, eagle-eyed for anything suspicious.

This is what Tim had been doing when he was killed. I'd been out on an escort mission when the news came in to get back to base. A suicide truckdriver had tried to crash the gate and Tim's interventions had been successful in keeping the vehicle out but it came at the cost of his life. We could never let our guard down over here...enemies came in all shapes and sizes.

Paired with Roscoe, we walked the front wall of the base and back again. We were not the only two assigned this duty as we kept a constant vigil as vehicles were moving through the gates. The wind was biting as it hit our cheeks, but I preferred this time of year over the blistering hot summer. At least now, my uniform kept most of me warm. We talked, but our eyes continually scanned the area, never letting our guard down.

"You made your plans yet?" he asked.

"Heading back home first to check on the family," I replied. A group of children ran over and we stopped to pass out candy, watching as they scampered off, chattering happily.

"You got a girl back home?"

I hesitated a beat too long, sparking his interest as he turned to eye me with a grin on his face. "You've been getting some letters and packages recently and not just from your mama. I'd say there's someone back home waitin' on you," he surmised, his wide smile of perfectly white teeth in stark contrast to his ebony skin.

Shaking my head while chuckling, I admitted, "Got a girl I'm interested in, but who knows how she feels."

"How long have you known her?"

Feeling foolish, I admitted, "Not long. I actually just met her when I escorted Tim's body back to his hometown."

That captured Roscoe's attention as he visible startled, his gaze rested on me for a few seconds before scanning the area again. "Damn, man. You meet a girl at a funeral and she's writing you letters? You must move fast!"

"Hell, it wasn't like that!" I protested. Seeing his eyebrow lift in question, I explained, "She was in the cemetery and I actually thought something was wrong. I went over after Tim's service to check on her."

Roscoe's voice changed as he asked, "Was she all right?"

"Yeah, it turns out she was visiting the gravesite of her fiancé who'd been killed six months ago while serving in the Army."

"No shit?"

Nodding as we turned the corner, I continued. "Crazy right? But we talked for a few minutes and I really didn't want to go over to Tim's parent's house...and...well, I liked talking to Becky. She was pretty but sort-of fragile. There was just something about her that called to me. So I asked her to coffee." Passing another pair of guards, we continued along the front wall after our acknowledgements.

"And?" Roscoe prodded.

Shrugging, I said, "Not much else to tell. We had a nice chat and the hour I spent with her just made me want to get to know her more."

"Love at first sight kind-of shit?" he joked.

Shaking my head at his taunts, knowing if I heard this

from someone else I'd probably think the same thing. "Not love at first sight. Definitely lust but, honestly, it's a whole lot more. I hated having to leave but got her email address and we've been corresponding ever since."

Roscoe was quiet a moment as though he was pondering my tale. "Well, you ain't got too much longer before you can get back and find out exactly how she feels," he replied, then shot me a stare. "But then you don't want to lose your chance, so maybe you'd better jump on it before someone else steps in."

As we continued to walk the dusty road, our gazes trained on the area around us, my mind mulled over his words.

That night, I slipped away from the poker game going on in my tent, feeling the tent walls closing in on me. Wandering the base in the dark of night, I always felt closer to home. The rows of tents were still very visible, but when I found a quiet corner and lifted my eyes to the stars in the inky sky, I could almost pretend I was back in West Virginia. And that made me feel closer to Becky.

My high school buddies and I used to hike in some of the mountain areas and camp underneath the stars. I closed my eyes for a moment, pretending to be underneath the stars on one of my favorite trails with her. *I had encouraged her to learn to move on to her future...but the truth was, I want to be her future.*

* * *

Picking up a letter at the mail tent, I was surprised to see the return address as Tim's mother. Wondering what she had to say, I ripped the envelope open. Pulling the stationary out, I unfolded the paper.

Dear Caleb,

I wanted to thank you once again for accompanying Tim's body home for burial. At the time, I was so full of my own grief, I'm not sure I acknowledged yours. He spoke of you often and I know the two of you were such good friends.

I wanted to let you know that I was placing fresh flowers on his gravesite yesterday and I met a friend of yours. Becky Adams came over to introduce herself to me. She told me that she met you after Tim's funeral and the two of you had a chance to talk. I am so glad. While I don't know Becky, I knew her mother through a committee we worked on for a local charity. I remember when Becky's fiancé was killed in action and how distraught her mother was. She was worried sick about Becky and, of course, at that time I had not experienced the horrible effects of grief yet.

But seeing Becky yesterday reminded me that we do move on...never forgetting, but finding a new path.

Tim used to talk about the two of you working together after you both finished your tours with the Army. And I just wanted to say that I hope you know that even though Tim won't be by your side, in spirit he'll be right beside you, cheering you on all the way.

I know I might be sticking my nose in where it doesn't belong, but I wanted to let you know that when Becky spoke of you yesterday, she was absolutely beaming. And somehow driving home from the cemetery, I could just see Tim smiling from above, thinking he brought the two of you together.

Please be safe,

Ellen Scarsdale

Stuffing the stationary back into the envelope, a wide grin spread across my face. With a mental fist-pump, I called out, "Thanks ol' buddy!" just before heading back into the tent. And somehow, I knew Tim heard me.

CHAPTER 6

(FEBRUARY – BECKY)

How exciting—filling out the online graduation information for the university made the end of my impending student status feel real. I'd been busy applying for teaching jobs but with an uncertain economy, I knew I had to cast my net wide. I didn't mind moving to another state but didn't want to be too far from my parents.

The thought of moving away and finding a new apartment no longer filled me with dread—instead I was looking forward to moving out of my old room. In fact, I'd just teased mom about her finally having the guest room back.

Smiling at a few friends as I walked along the row of tables in the university library, I settled in a corner study booth, preferring the quiet environment. Pulling up my emails, I was pleased to see a few from some of my job inquiries. Clicking on them one at a time, I heaved a frustrated sigh as each one promised to get back with me once their budgets were set. *Okay, so that's not a "no" but so far they hadn't asked me for an interview yet.*

Tucking my hair behind my ear, I sighed as I continued

to fill out applications, saying a little prayer every time I hit send.

"Hey, Becky!"

Turning, I smiled at one of my friends, also in the education program. "Congratulations on your job offer. I heard you decided to head to D.C." I was sincere, but had to admit I was also envious.

Sidney, a pretty brunette, plopped into the chair across from me and offered a tired smile. "Thanks. Yeah, with Craig getting a job for a lobbyist group, I decided to try for a teaching position there. Being an inner-city elementary school, it'll be different from what I expected, but they need teachers desperately."

"So when's the wedding?"

Her gaze jumped to mine, a slight blush staining her cheeks. "Um...this summer."

I reached over and touched her arm. "Sidney, you don't have to be embarrassed. I'm happy for you and Craig."

Her gaze dropped to my left hand and she bit her lip before nodding slightly toward my empty ring finger. "I notice you don't wear your engagement ring anymore," she said softly.

Sighing, I nodded. "Well, I finally realized that Robbie's not coming home to me...we're not getting married...and I'm technically not engaged. So, the time eventually came where I could take it off and not feel as though I was being unfaithful."

"Oh, honey, I'm so sorry," she said, her eyes full of sympathy.

Smiling softly, I replied, "I'm going to be fine...really. I have no idea what the future holds, but I'm finally looking forward instead of backward now."

Standing, she leaned over and offered me a hug before moving on toward the library elevators. Hearing the ding of an incoming email, I dreaded seeing another rejection but was elated to see another email from Caleb.

Becky,

I just got off a long shift and wanted to email you before I headed to the DFAC. That's the name of our dining facility. I figured once I ate, all I'd want to do is go back to the tent and crash.

I've been thinking of what I want to do as soon as I get out of the military now that my plans with Tim are no longer in my future. I really think that I want to pursue becoming a private investigator and have been checking into the requirements. I could work with an established firm and then eventually branch out into my own business. I've spent the past six years in the Army and it'll be weird not being a soldier anymore. But I'm ready for a change.

I was thinking of the changes you've had to have this past year and just want to tell you how brave I think you are. I know sometimes you don't feel strong, but you really are. You're grieving but moving forward. I'm really proud of you and honored to call you a friend.

I got a letter from Tim's mom telling me that she met you on a visit to the cemetery. She said it was really nice talking to you and was glad that we had met. She also said that as she was driving home, she felt that Tim would be smiling at bringing us together that day.

I just want to let you know that meeting you that day in the cemetery was life changing for me. I want us to meet up again when I get out. I was telling a friend about you and they thought I should go ahead and made some plans so that I don't let you slip through my fingers. So let me ask you out now before your social calendar fills up!

I'd love to take you to dinner instead of just a quick cup of coffee. I've loved getting to know you through letters and emails, but I really want to see you in person. It won't be long until I'm back in the states – only one more month. I'll visit my folks first and then I'll make it to you...if you'll agree to go on a date with me...the first of what I hope will be many.

Love,
Caleb

Unable to hold back the smile, I re-read his email again. *He wants to take me to dinner!* I haven't been on a date since Robbie's death. A few friends had hinted that they had men they could set me up with, but I had no desire for a blind date...or worse, a pity date. But knowing Caleb desired to see me again was just what I wanted to hear since I wanted to see him also.

Another sound from my computer alerted an incoming email. A quick glance indicated it was from one of the counties I had applied for a teaching position. Hesitating for a second, I clicked on the link. Gasping as I read, my heart leaped as they offered me an interview. Asking me to visit next month during my spring semester break, I couldn't hit the accept button fast enough. *Yes, yes, yes!*

Feeling lighter than I had in a long time, I closed my laptop and headed through the cold wind to my car. An hour later, over dinner, I shared about the interview with my parents.

"Oh, honey, that's wonderful," mom gushed. "I just wish it were closer."

"I know, but it's not far, I promise. It's just over the state line."

"I think that's a fairly poor economic area," her father commented, his brows drawn down.

Nodding, I agreed. "Yeah, I looked them up and it is. I think that's why they need teachers. But, they've received a grant so they can offer a competitive salary for new teachers. And it won't be hard to find housing there." Shrugging, I added, "It doesn't have to be forever, but I'd love to start out somewhere I can be appreciated."

My gaze bounced between mom and dad, watching as the concern in their eyes slowly change as smiles curved their lips. It was heartening to finally be able to make them smile again. Dad reached across the table and grasped my hand.

"Becky, your mom and I are so proud of you. You've managed to grieve, hold on to the special memories of Robbie and what you had planned, but have also been able to slowly move forward, finding that there is still so much life for you."

"And," mom quickly added, "that it's okay to have that life...without guilt. I know Robbie would want that for you."

Tears sprang to my eyes as I offered a watery smile in return.

* * *

The air was crisp but the sun shone gloriously in the bright blue sky. Still snuggling in my winter coat as I walked up the cemetery hill, I welcomed the milder weather. Making my way to Robbie's gravesite, I took my usual place on the marble bench. Facing his stone, I sucked in a deep breath, letting it out slowly.

"Well, Robbie, it's been a couple of weeks since I've been here. Midterms are upon me and I've spent a lot of time in the library. You know, I'm almost finished with my degree." A soft smile slipped out as I remembered how supportive he was of my attending college.

"You used to tell me that I'd make a good teacher and I guess we'll find out, won't we?" I reached up to my neck and pulled out the gold necklace, clasping my engagement ring dangling on the delicate chain. Holding it tightly in my hand, I closed my eyes.

"Oh, Robbie, I've got a chance to have a teaching job but I'd have to move away. Not too far, but I wouldn't be able to come every week to talk to you. At least not here."

Opening my eyes once more, I stared at the grey, marble slab in front of me, each inch of it memorized. "I know it's baby-steps, but I feel like I need some kind of sign from you that this is the right thing to do."

I sat for several more minutes but the only sounds were the breeze blowing through the evergreen trees lining the edge of the cemetery. No voices. No words of wisdom. No butterflies or doves flying. No sign.

Sighing as I rose from the bench, I stepped forward and kneeled at his stone, my right hand plastered to the front as my fingers traced his engraved name for the millionth time. "I'll always love you, Robbie," I whispered. "No matter where I go, or who I'm with, a part of me will always carry you in my heart." Bending over, I kissed the stone...the cold, silent marble meeting my lips.

With a deep breath, I stood and walked back down the hill.

* * *

(Caleb)

Another day on the job, but as I walked around each vehicle coming onto the base with my long-stick mirror in my hands checking for hidden bombs, I worked to keep my focus on the job and not on counting down the days left until I could go home.

Roscoe rounded the other side, giving the all-clear sign. Checked on my side as well, we waved to the driver, signaling for him to drive through. Grinning, Roscoe made a grand gesture of checking his watch. "Hmmm, how many days you got here, bro?"

"Five days, eleven hours, and about thirty-five minutes until my plane takes off," I called out, earning a raised-eyebrow look from him.

"Damn man, I knew you had it down, but that was impressive!" he laughed. "So, you got plans for that sweet thing whose picture you've got taped to your bunk?"

Nodding, I clapped him on the back and replied, "Hell yeah. Gonna go see my parents first and then make it over to her place. I did what you suggested and already made a date with her. I've checked on what I'll need for my PI license in her state and I plan on taking her out for a huge steak dinner for our first date."

Roscoe threw his head back in laughter before slapping me on the shoulder. "That's my man. Too much fuckin' time gets wasted over here, so you gotta make up for it!"

Just then the next vehicle pulled up and we began our careful inspection once more.

Two hours later, I ran by the MWR to see if I had another email from Becky. Pulling up one from my dad, I clicked.

Son,

Your mom and I can't wait to have you home again. We've had a bit of a setback and while your mom doesn't want you to know this now, she's having some health issues. She's had some chest pain and her doctor is running tests on her heart. You know her—she'd be angry at me for sending this email, but I know you'd like to pray for her and that you need to be prepared.

You come home in less than a week, and I gotta say it'll be great to have you home again. We are counting down the days. Seeing you again will really perk your mom up (I think she's more worried than she lets on). Take care, son and stay safe.

Love,
Dad

I read and re-read the email over several times, my eyes not believing the words dad had written. Dad was strong but mom had always been the rock in the family. The idea of her being ill was as foreign to me as this land I was in.

Sucking in a deep breath, I said a prayer for her health, working to keep the fear from my heart. Leaning back in my chair, I also knew that my future had changed once more. There was no way I could move closer to Becky...at least not now. Not when my parents might need me.

My heart heavy, for my mom and for my possible derailed career and relationship plans, my fingers hovered over the keys momentarily. Finally, pulling my thoughts other I began to type.

Becky,

I just got an email from my dad, and mom is having

to have some medical tests done. I only know it has to do with her heart and once I get home next week I'll have more information. I'm worried about her but thankful this didn't happen when I first got here. At least I'll see her soon.

But I can't make any firm plans until I know what is going on with her. Please don't think this is my attempt to change our plans or get out of seeing you! My heart is pulled, both knowing my parents need me and that I want to come to you as soon as possible.

I'm sending you my phone number and hope you'll send me yours too. That way we can call/text until I'll be able to visit.

I've been counting down the days and that hasn't changed. The steak dinner will be just a little postponed, I promise!

Love,
Caleb

CHAPTER 7

(MARCH – CALEB)

"Mom, seriously, I can't eat another bite."

"Caleb, let me spoil you," she protested, heaping another piece of chocolate cake onto my dessert plate.

I looked to dad for support, but he threw his hands up and said, "Son, you've been home just a few hours and your mom's been cooking for a week. You're gonna be eating like this for a while!"

I'd made it back to the states, finished my Army outprocessing, and now...I was spending my first day as a civilian back with my parents. I'd emailed Becky as soon as I was able a few days ago, but knew I had to bide my time before I could visit. She was on a trip during her midterm break and said she had a job interview. Just thinking of her sent a smile across my face.

"So what do you have planned now that you're out?" dad asked.

"Joshua," mom fussed. "Give the boy a chance to breath! I just want to enjoy having him home."

"No, it's okay," I assured. "I'm starting online classes for investigations and plan on attending the required course for becoming licensed as a private investigator."

"Oh, are you staying here?" Mom's eyes lit at the idea of me not moving away. She knew dad had told me about her health and it was obvious she gained comfort having me close by.

Ducking my head, I confessed, "For now. I want to be around for you all and well, then we'll see."

Mom's face clouded for a moment before she leaned over and placed her hand on my arm. "Caleb, as much as I would love to have you near, I don't expect you to stay here."

I laid my hand on hers and shook my head slowly. "Mom, right now, I want to be close by until we know more about what's going on with you. I'm staying for now and can do the online classes from here."

I knew her eyes were on me, but I could not think of anything to say to deflect before she asked, "Why do I get the feeling that you've got something else going on?"

Seeing both mom and dad's gazes now firmly planted on me, I rubbed my hand over my face as I sighed. "Well, to be honest, I met someone in Virginia when I came back for Tim's funeral. We've been corresponding and I plan on trying to see her sometime. I don't know how things will end up, but I'd like to have the chance to see where they will go."

Both parents were silent but as I lifted my gaze, I saw smiles on their faces. My dad just nodded approvingly and mom's grin spread wide. "So what's stopping you?" mom asked.

Hesitating in my answer for a moment too long, mom jumped in. "You are not going to stay here just for me!" Her eyes were snapping as she sat up straight, her lips pressed together in a tight line.

Throwing my hands up, I replied, "Hey, she's got midterms now anyway, so there's no hurry. And I promise," leaning over to kiss mom's cheek, "to see her just as soon as it works out."

That night, I sent a text to Becky as I lay in bed. **Hope your interview is a success. Can't wait to hear about it. This is my first night as a civilian and I can't help but wish I were with you.**

A few minutes later a reply came back. **I'm so proud of you. I will only be gone two days and then I'll be back home. Wish me luck on the interview.**

Loving the fact that we could text and not just rely on email, I fired off another one. **I wish you all the luck in the world, but anyone would be fortunate to have you. Including me.**

No reply came back and my stomach dropped. *Was that too much? Too soon? Damn, I should have kept it light.* Fearing I had screwed up, my eyes jumped to the phone screen as it vibrated.

I can't wait to see you again! <3

With a lighter heart, I lay in my old bed in my childhood room and thought of the future. One that I planned on including Becky.

* * *

The next afternoon after meeting with a security and investigations company based in Elkins, I stepped out into the early spring sunshine, inhaling the fresh, mountain air. The company was interested in me, with my background in Military Police. Now, I just had to get my PI license and they'd take me on for my probationary period. I wanted to text Becky and tell her the news, but was afraid she was in her interview. *I'll wait till tonight.*

The thought of her slowed my steps and was the only threat to my day's success. I wanted to be near her, but knew I needed to proceed with my career and see how mom was. Once I finished the training, certification, and probation as a PI, then I could move to wherever she was. Only one more year and I vowed to see her as often as I could during that time. Lifting my head in determination, I continued toward my Jeep.

"Caleb? Caleb!"

I turned, hearing my name, my gaze scanning the sidewalk for someone familiar, landing on a beautiful face. *Becky? No way...what is she doing here?*

Dressed in black slacks and a heavy grey jacket with a light pink blouse peeking from the collar, her long blonde hair hung down her back, pulled away from her face with just a pink headband. Her cheeks were rosy with the slight chill in the air and her eyes twinkled in a way I had not witness when we first met.

As she trotted toward me in her heels, I hustled to meet her. Throwing my arms out instinctively, she ran straight into me, her arms encircling my waist as I drew her near. Inhaling the sweet scent of her hair, I closed my eyes for a second, wondering if this was a dream. Pulling back slightly, I held her at arms length, drinking her in. "What are you doing here?"

Grinning, she replied, "This is where my job interview was. Well, near here. It's actually about thirty minutes away but I had a college friend from here and spent the night with her. I was just about to leave."

Looking at her beautiful face beaming up toward me, I couldn't believe my luck. "You're coming here to work?"

Shrugging slightly, she said, "Well, they offered me the job. It's in Pendleton County." Cocking her head to the side, she asked, "What are you doing here?'

"Becky...that's where I'm from," I stammered, my heart pounding. Her eyes grew wide as I watched her smile light my world. Not wanting to have our reunion interrupted, I rushed, "Do you want to have dinner. Now? With me?"

Laughing, she nodded. "Oh, absolutely," she replied. "I'd like that."

Remembering what I told Roscoe, I drove us to the best restaurant in town, placing my hand on her lower back as I escorted her in proudly. Grateful the hostess glanced between the two of us with a smile on her face, as though she knew this was a special occasion, and led us to a corner table overlooking the mountains in the background.

After ordering, we sat for a moment not speaking, our gazes locked in on each other. Jolting when the waitress brought our drinks, we both laughed.

She broke the silence first, asking, "How's your mom?"

"Actually, she'll be having more tests this week, but her doctor thinks she's better." Lost in her gaze, I confessed, "This isn't how I expected things to go, Becky. I'd planned on coming home for just a week and then coming to see you, but I'm needed here right now—"

She reached over and placed her hand on top of mine offering a little squeeze. "Oh, Caleb, don't apologize! I understand...your place is with your family right now. And...well...uh...with my new job offer, I'll be in the area, so...uh..."

I saw her hesitation and finishing her sentence for her, I grinned, "So we can be together here."

Her wide smile beamed on me as she nodded. "Yeah. Funny how that worked out, huh?"

"Like it was meant to be."

The meal ended much too quickly and I reluctantly dropped her off at her car. I jogged over to open her door, offering my hand. Once more, warmth spread throughout me as her fingers entwined with mine.

Standing between our two vehicles, I pressed her back gently against her car, watching carefully to make sure she wanted this as much as I did. Making it easy on me, she grabbed my cheeks, pulling me down for a kiss.

I let her have control for a moment before taking ownership. With one hand at the back of her neck and the other on her jaw, I angled her head for maximum contact. It began as the soft exploration of a first kiss but then quickly exploded into white hot need. As she moaned into my mouth, I slipped my tongue inside her warmth as I felt her body shiver. Uncertain her legs would hold her, I slid my hand to her waist, holding tightly. With my fingers digging into her hips, I felt hers on my shoulders. Each touch seemed to burn us both as the flames of desire coursed all around us.

I wanted so much more than just a kiss but standing on the street was not the place to entertain those thoughts. Slowing the intensity of our tangled tongues, I licked and nipped her lips as we gradually separated. Cupping the back of her head against my pounding heartbeat, we stood for several silent minutes, each lost in our own thoughts and desires.

Loosening my grip, we separated just a few inches allowing me to peer into her eyes, making sure she was all right. Lighting her beautiful face, her beaming smile greeted me. "You okay?" I asked.

Nodding, with a slight blush staining her cheeks, she replied, "More than all right."

Not holding back, I confessed, "I hate letting you go."

Licking her lips, she offered, "I can come back next weekend. I only have two more months until I graduate and then I'll have to find a place to live around here. Um… maybe you can help me with that."

Grinning, my heart lighter than in months, I agreed. "Can't think of anything better."

With a final goodbye kiss, I watched as she settled in her car. Waving until she was no longer in sight, I got in my truck, my dog-tags hanging around the rear-view mirror. Thinking of my friend, I said, "You'd like her, Tim."

* * *

(July - Becky)

"You'd like him, Robbie."

With the warm summer sun on my back, I kneeled once more at the gravestone. White, billowy clouds floated through the blue sky, and the lush, green grass underneath my knees provided a cushion. I rested my fingers gently on the marble, tracing his name as I talked to him. "He's kind and good and he loves me. He makes me laugh. He makes my heart sing once more." Standing, I smiled down at the site that had held my body as it shook with sobs of anguish and gave me peace. "I asked for a sign, didn't I? And when I least expected it, you gave it to me. He and I ended up in the same place."

Bending over, I kissed the stone, recognizing the twinge of sadness at the tragic passing of someone so young and the changes in my life. Sucking in a cleansing breath, I let it out slowly. "I'll see you the next time I'm home, Robbie. All my love…"

Turning, I began the walk down the cemetery knoll toward the handsome man waiting patiently at the bottom of the hill. Glancing down at the new engagement ring on my finger, the twin diamonds sparkling. Caleb had taken the diamond from Robbie's ring and had it made into a gorgeous ring with a matching diamond. He said it represented the love of my past and the love of my future.

Lifting my gaze as I came closer to him, he grinned as he stepped toward me. Wrapping me in his embrace, he peered into my face. "You okay, babe?" he asked, his eyes searching mine.

Nodding, I assured, "Yeah. I'm at peace...with Robbie and with you."

"I'm glad," he said, leaning over to meet my lips. Kissing me deeply, we separated reluctantly. Arms around each other we walked toward our future.

Don't miss any news about new releases! Sign up for my Newsletter
For the next Letters From Home book:
Freedom of Love
Bond of Love

Other Books by Maryann Jordan
Alvarez Security
Gabe
Tony
Vinny
Jobe

Love's Series
Love's Taming
Love's Tempting
Love's Trusting

Saints Protection & Investigations
(an elite group, assigned to the cases no one else wants…or can solve)
Serial Love
Healing Love
Revealing Love
Seeing Love
Honor Love
Sacrifice Love
Protecting Love
Remember Love
Discover Love
Surviving Love
Celebrating Love

The Baytown Boys Series
Coming Home
Just One More Chance
Clues of the Heart
Finding Peace

The Fairfield Series
(small town detectives and the women they love)
Laurie's Time
Carol's Image
Emma's Home
Fireworks Over Fairfield

Please take the time to leave a review of this book.
Feel free to contact me, especially if you enjoyed my book.
I love to hear from readers!
Facebook
Email
Website

Made in United States
Orlando, FL
08 March 2022

15533343R00107